"Should we spend more time together?"

Sean's voice was soft as he continued, "Is that what you'd like?"

"No!" Rowena cried, horrified. "I mean, I'm quite happy with the present arrangements," she babbled, panicky at the thought of being constantly alone in his company.

"Are you afraid of me?" he demanded, and she felt her cheeks grow pink under his steady gaze.

How on earth could she answer that, Rowena wondered. If he wanted the truth, it was yes; she was afraid of what he could do to her emotions. Afraid of her reaction, because she was still attracted to him in spite of everything. "Of course not!" she managed to get out indignantly.

"I'm almost inclined to put that to a proper test," Sean said quietly, his blue eyes searing into Rowena's startled brown ones.

JANE CORRIE
is also the author of these
Harlequin Romances

Many of these titles are available at your local bookseller.

For a free catalogue listing all available Harlequin Romances
and Harlequin Presents, send your name and address to:

HARLEQUIN READER SERVICE
1440 South Priest Drive, Tempe, AZ 85281
Canadian address: Stratford, Ontario N5A 6W2

Bride
for Sale

by

JANE CORRIE

Harlequin Books

TORONTO • LONDON • LOS ANGELES • AMSTERDAM
SYDNEY • HAMBURG • PARIS • STOCKHOLM • ATHENS • TOKYO

Original hardcover edition published in 1981
by Mills & Boon Limited

ISBN 0-373-02431-2

Harlequin edition published October 1981

Printed in U.S.A.

CHAPTER ONE

'YES, well, you know what your father wants, don't you?' said Sean Tancred, his blue eyes piercing Rowena Southall's startled brown ones. Not that she was startled, she knew exactly what her father wanted, but the look was part of Rowena's make-up, owing to a slight eye malfunction that gave her large eyes a questing, almost frightened look as she gazed back at the tall, handsome man who was now staring out of the drawing room window.

Her gaze followed his out to the immaculately lawned area surrounding the house, but she said nothing; there was nothing she could say.

'Put him up to it, did you?' Sean asked sharply, directing his attention back to the watching Rowena.

She took a deep breath and shook her head. If she said no, he wouldn't believe her, and she looked away from his blue stare that seemed to go right through her. She hated her father for putting her in this position. It was bad enough being on offer, like a box of cornflakes on the grocer's shelf, without having to witness the customer's bald rejection of such an offer, or the disdain she was now being subjected to.

'Lost your tongue?' he taunted. 'Well, I'm not surprised. It takes a lot to throw me, but I'll admit——' He turned away from the window abruptly. 'I've decided to accept his offer,' he announced bluntly. 'He drove a hard bargain,' he went on, his finely moulded lips curling at the recollection of his interview with Gerald Southall earlier that morning, 'but when the devil drives,' he gave a shrug and turned to face the cringing Rowena who had given a wince at his bald summing-up of the position. 'You'll forgive me for forgoing the usual trite utterances, I'm sure,' he added harshly. 'Money can buy a lot of things, and I want a lot of it right now to put Tancred House to rights, and that's what you've bought—nothing else—I trust you understand me? You'll have my name, and your father will get that coveted entrée into my clubs, but that's as far as it goes. I don't know what you'll find to do at Tancred House, but whatever it is, please do not expect me to participate in any activity. As I've said, money can buy a lot of things, but there are things it can't buy,' he acknowledged Rowena's deep blush with a twisted sneer. 'I see you understand me,' he said harshly, and walked to the door. 'I'll see myself out,' he announced grandly, and a moment later he had gone, leaving Rowena staring at her tightly clenched hands.

A moment later the door opened again and Gerald Southall walked in. He was vastly pleased with himself, it was in his voice as he said, 'The knot's as good as tied, girl. I knew he wouldn't turn it down. I consider myself a good judge of men,' he went on smugly, 'had him taped from the start, for all his high and mighty ways there's nothing he wouldn't do to save that estate. It'll cost a pretty penny, mind you, but worth it,' he added musingly, and glanced at his daughter, who stood with closed eyes looking exactly as she felt, as if wanting to put a hand over her ears to blot out her father's words. 'You can stop looking as if the end of the world's come!' he snapped at her. 'You've got the pick of the county. My only regret is that I couldn't persuade him to take up the title again—still,' he added thoughtfully, 'the name's still there, and that counts for something. My grandsons won't be called "the grocer's boys", and that's good enough for me.'

'There won't be any grandsons,' Rowena managed to get out, trying unsuccessfully to control her voice and prevent herself from shouting the words at him. 'You've bought the house, and the name, and that's all—and we mustn't forget the admittance to the golf club and his London clubs, must we?' she added almost hysterically.

Gerald Southall waved this announcement away with an impatience that was characteristic of him. 'Not right away, of course. But he'll accept it, you'll see. He's a man, isn't he? You've not got your mother's looks, but you're passable for all that. There are ways,' he stated comfortably, 'and no doubt you'll find how to go about it,' and at Rowena's wild shake of the head he added exasperatedly, 'and don't try to tell me different. I've seen the moony looks you've sent him, and the way you used to flush up if he looked your way.'

Rowena stared down at her hands, clenched tightly together, but did not refute this statement. It was true that she had had a crush on Sean Tancred, but 'had' was the operative word; she was no longer the shy seventeen-year-old who had earned herself the nickname of 'Miss Mouse' to Sean and his friends. She took an inward breath. It would be useless to point this out to her father, he wouldn't believe her, simply because he didn't want his plans disrupted.

Gerald Southall gave her an exasperated look and shrugged his broad shoulders. 'I don't know why I bother!' he said irritably. 'There's four girls that I know of in the village who would jump at the chance that you're being given. He hasn't asked any of them to marry him, has he?' he demanded. 'He's going on for thirty now and it's time he settled down. He's the last of his line and he'll want heirs.' He stared out of the window, but his eyes were not on the view. 'So we're not out of the top drawer, but we've brass, lass, and that's what counts. It wouldn't be the first time that it's happened. Look back at the past, there's many a snooty landowner that's settled for a girl with a fortune. Pride's all very well, but it doesn't pay the bills, does it? It's not as if he were buying a pig in a poke, either,' he went on musingly, unaware of Rowena's wince at his North-country brashness. 'You've had the best education possible—aye, even better than that Diana Fisher who's always hanging round the hall, for all her airs and graces. You're as good as she is, and don't you forget it.' On this sharp directive he left Rowena to the peace and solitude she had longed for after her painful interlude with the man that she was going to marry.

At this point of time in her life there was not a lot that Rowena had to be grateful about, in spite of her father's bald summing-up of the situation, but she was grateful that Sean Tancred did not intend to humiliate her further by making a token consummation of the marriage. She was also grateful that he had made this plain to her father right from the start of the marriage contract, so that he could not blame her if his hopes of grand-children did not materialise.

Only he would blame her, she thought mis-erably, just as he had blamed her for encouraging David to take up art and turn his back on the gro-cery trade. Her eyes went to the wall opposite her and rested fondly on a small painting of a land-scape. No matter what it had cost her, she would have stood by her brother, who, she was con-vinced, would one day make his name in the world of art.

Her eyes traced the delicately painted woodland scene of the picture, remembering how she had tried to point out to her father how talented his only son was, and how dreadful it would be if he refused him the chance of studying at one of the best art schools in the country.

She sighed. Her father had no eye for beauty, not unless it made a fat profit, and to pay out what he called 'good brass, for nought,' was un-heard-of.

Rowena gave a twisted smile as she recalled her joy at having won the battle over David's future, bridging the gap between father and son, and taking all the brickbats such a position heralded. David had a lot of his mother in him, his gift of painting had been inherited from her, for she had been a fine watercolour painter before she had married Gerald Southall and had been forced to drop all pretensions to becoming successful in her chosen career after her marriage.

Only Rowena had known how much this had meant to her mother, who had come from a quiet farming family in the dales of Yorkshire, and who had wanted nothing more than a country scene before her and a sketching pad in her hands. Rowena gave a deep sigh. Her mother had met her father at a training college, where she was studying art, and Gerald Southall was on a management course.

Rowena looked back at the view out of the windows. Whatever else could be levelled at her father, he had known what he wanted, and set about achieving it. There were no half-measures where he was concerned. He was ambitious, and determined to make his mark in the world of trade, and he had done so in no small way. He now owned a chain of grocery stores that stretched across the country and had become a household name. All this he had achieved from one small store his father had left him, and whom he had helped to run the store since he was old enough to reach the top of the serving counter.

He was a self-made tycoon, and proud of the fact, and not slow in boasting of his progress to his less successful colleagues. Not unnaturally this made him unpopular with a great many people and he had few friends. Those he did have, Rowena suspected, were purely hangers-on, hoping that some of the vast profits might land in their direction. Her mother, with the inbred directness of North-country folk, had heartily disliked most of her husband's friends, for she saw beyond their flattering comments.

Rowena stared at the framed photograph of her mother on a small side table. She would have liked this house, she thought, with its views of the rolling downs of Sussex, so vastly different from the grand house in London that they had lived in before she had died four years ago. She sighed restlessly. If only her father had listened to her mother's request that they move out of London and settle in this quiet backwater village of Knight's Gate, that had caught her fancy while on a visit to a friend of hers, but Gerald Southall had not been ready to leave the hubbub of city life at that time, and had given a vague promise to the effect that perhaps one day they would do just that.

Julia Southall had had to be content with this, but she made a point of visiting Knight's Gate as often as she was able to. Her college friend, now a teacher in the local school, gave her a good excuse for her visits and she always took Rowena and David with her, to give them, as she put it, a breath of good country air.

Her death four years ago had been entirely unpredictable, when the slight cold that she had caught turned to bronchitis, that in a matter of days had become pneumonia, and within a week eighteen-year-old Rowena and seventeen-year-old David had lost their mother.

Precisely one year later Gerald Southall moved his family out of London to Knight's Gate, and bought Eagles' Roost, a fine old country house in the heart of the village.

The news that they were going to live in Knight's Gate had at first filled both Rowena and David with dismay, for it would bring back memories they were trying to forget, but Rowena's timid comments on these sentiments were brushed aside by her father with a bald, 'It's what your mother would have wanted,' and that was that, and Rowena's sad thought that if he had done what her mother wanted a few years earlier they might not have lost her made the proposed move all the more poignant.

There was but one consolation for her in the move, and that was that she would no longer have to face those social occasions that had cropped up so often in London, where she would have to stand in for her mother and act as hostess, handing round the sherry and making desultory conversation with her father's business colleagues.

As his private secretary, she had been fully occupied and kept up to date with business affairs. She was intelligent and utterly reliable, and although her father never said so, she knew he was satisfied with her contribution to the family business.

David, however, was a constant source of irritation to his father. His school reports were far from brilliant, and no amount of threats or bribery would alter his progress. The sad fact of the matter was that he had set his heart on becoming an artist and no other subject interested him.

Rowena had lost count of the rows they had had. The angrier her father became, the more stubborn David became. Only in certain subjects did David shine, and of course they were the subjects that he had to pass in order to get to art school. This very fact acted like a red rag to a bull to his father, for it emphasised the boy's determined stand on his chosen career, proving to the frustrated Gerald Southall that he had ample ability to shine in the business world if he would only put his mind to it.

It was through Rowena that David had won the day, and had been allowed to go to art school. She had shamelessly worked on her father's one weak spot in his make-up—his pride. He had never forgotten his early days as the village shop lad, expected to touch his cap to his superiors, as taught him by his wily father who saw no harm in bestowing such currying favours on his more wealthy customers, but it had left a mark of inferiority on the young Gerald that he had fought all his life to overcome.

Her campaign had been helped by the fact that an old adversary of her father's, namely Sir George Hadden, whose knighthood had been granted solely on his business prowess that had enabled him to give generous grants to popular charities, also had a son who aspired to become an artist, but had failed to reach the necessary standard for acceptance at the famous London art school. As she had pointed out this salient fact, she had known that the battle was won by the light of sheer satisfaction that she saw in her father's eyes, as he envisaged meeting Sir George at some future function and wiping what he had often called his self-satisfied smirk off his florid face.

There was a knock on the door at this point, and Mrs Gany, the housekeeper, entered with a tray of coffee. 'Mr Southall's on the phone,' she said to Rowena, 'so I left his coffee on the table by the study door.' She smiled in a conspiratorial fashion at Rowena. 'I didn't feel like being shouted at today,' she added, 'so I didn't risk it.'

As the door closed behind her Rowena sighed and poured herself out a cup of coffee. Her father did shout, even in normal conversation. He always had done, and she had often vaguely wondered if it had anything to do with the mills, for it seemed to be characteristic of North-country folk, although her father's family had had nothing to do with the textile industry.

Rowena carried her coffee over to the window seat and settled down to her musings again. Her so-called victory over David's future had been of short duration, and she ought to have known that her father would find some way to capitalise on it, but had never dreamed of finding herself offered as a sacrificial lamb on the altar of his ambition to become accepted by the gentry.

Rowena's hand holding her cup shook as she placed it back in the saucer again. She had never dreamed that Sean Tancred would accept such an incredible proposal as the one her father had put to him that morning, either, but he had, and Rowena was still trying to assimilate this bald and entirely unfeasible fact.

She shook her head, making her dark hair bounce away from her face and spring back again, and she brushed away a clinging strand of hair with an action of impatience. This was the twentieth century, wasn't it? she asked herself bewilderedly. Marriages were not made like that in this day and age, she told herself firmly, but was completely unable to convince herself on this point.

Tancred House was medieval, she thought ironically, and so was Sean Tancred's approach to the situation. There were many such marriages in those times, as her father had been quick to point out to her, but none of that concerned her now, she only knew that if she refused to do what her father asked, David would suffer the consequences.

She closed her eyes as she went over the scene that morning in her father's study when she was supposed to be taking dictation, and he had thrown the news at her. She could still feel the shock waves as he had calmly informed her that he had decided to offer Sean Tancred a way out of his monetary problems caused by crippling death duties on the estate. In return for this generous gesture, Sean Tancred was to marry Rowena.

Rowena remembered just sitting there and staring at her father, certain that he had taken leave of his senses, but his curt nod of confirmation had dashed even this slight hope, and she felt waves of shame wash over her for his insensitivity in suggesting such an arrangement. 'By all means help him, if that's what you want to do,' she remembered replying dryly, not really able to believe that such a conversation was taking place, 'but you can't seriously expect him to accept on those conditions—and how——' she swallowed convulsively, 'you expect me to fall in line with such an outrageous suggestion is beyond my comprehension!' she ended indignantly.

Her father had calmly lit a cigar before replying airily, 'You'll get used to the idea after you've had time to think about it.'

'Get used to the idea?' Rowena had repeated in

a stunned voice. 'Get used to the fact that I'm being married off to a man I hardly know, simply because of his name and standing in high society—not that he'll agree, thank goodness,' she added as she took a deep breath. 'For goodness' sake, Father! This sort of arrangement went out with the Middle Ages. You'll only make a fool of yourself, and cause me no end of embarrassment.' She gave an inward groan as she saw the familiar signs of obstinacy in her father's face. 'Well, I'm warning you,' she added firmly. 'If you do go ahead, you're on your own. I'll have nothing whatsoever to do with it, and nothing will change my mind,' she stated adamantly.

Gerald Southall had stared down at his glowing cigar before saying harshly, 'Do you know why I retired early, Rowena?'

Rowena gave him a wary look and shrugged her slim shoulders. She had an idea what was coming next, but if he thought he was going to blackmail her on those premises he had another think coming. 'Because you'd had enough of city life, I presume,' she replied.

'Because my constitution had had enough of city life, to be precise,' he replied sourly, 'according to Dr Jenks, that is. Pack it in while you're still able to enjoy life, was his advice, and I took it.' His glance left his cigar and he looked up at Rowena. 'So here we are,' he stared round at the rich furnishings of the study. 'We've a fine house, but what else have we got, eh? Well, I'll tell you—nought! We're just the rich grocers on the hill to the locals, and only acknowledged when they want a subscription for the church fund or the village memorial. How many invitations do you get for the local do's?' he demanded caustically. 'Oh, aye,' he nodded sarcastically, 'they asked you to the garden fête, didn't they, and put you in charge of the jumble stall, suggesting at the same time how much they'd appreciate anything that you could come up with as they were rather short of merchandise. They didn't ask you to the fancy get-together tea party in Mrs Winthrop's house afterwards, did they? Said a nice "thank you" and left you to make your own way home.' His brown eyes narrowed in thought. 'It was raining by then, if I remember rightly,' he added, 'and you came in soaked to the skin. There was nothing to stop the Winthrop woman running you back, was there? She was only too happy to pick you up and take you out there.'

'She didn't know it was going to rain, did she?' Rowena remonstrated quietly. 'She only picked me up in the first place because I had some things for the stall, and it wasn't very far to walk. As for not being asked to the local functions—well, that's my own fault, I didn't exactly encourage them. I'm not very good at mixing with people; you know that. I don't really know anybody here, apart from Miss Heysham,' she added.

'Jenny Heysham's all right,' Gerald Southall begrudgingly admitted, 'but she was your mother's friend. You need friends of your own age, not a schoolteacher who's just retired.'

'But I'm perfectly happy as I am,' Rowena argued softly. 'The trouble is, you're bored with country life. Why don't you contact Mr Soper again? Or join that new golf club out at Pickerings? I'm sure they'd be only too pleased to have you on the membership.'

Gerald Southall had glared at his daughter. 'Second best,' he had growled. 'And since when have I accepted second best, eh? You tell me that. As for contacting Soper again, there's no point. No one's died that I know of, and the answer's always the same—full membership, and the usual cover-up about letting me know when there's a vacancy.' His eyes narrowed in speculation. 'I've a feeling I won't have too long to wait for that vacancy after your marriage to Sean Tancred,' he added musingly.

'If that's your only reason for going ahead with that preposterous suggestion, then it's simply not good enough!' Rowena had gasped, torn between an hysterical urge to laugh, or to reveal her shocked feelings on her father's bulldozing tactics to get what he wanted. 'And I'm sorry I can't oblige you.' She got up quickly from her chair to show him that she had had enough of what she considered to be a hypothetical situation, and made for the study door.

'Well, I only hope David settles down here as well as you have,' her father commented gruffly as she reached the door.

Rowena paused in the act of opening the door and turned to face her father. 'David?' she said in a puzzled voice. 'He's not due home until the Easter recess—and not even then,' she added, smiling. 'I believe he's decided to join some friends of his on a sketching holiday in the Highlands.'

Her father gave a shrug as if to say that this was irrelevant information. 'He's a few weeks, I sup-

pose, in which to make his mind up about that
sort of thing, when he's decided to settle for a
steady job. He's played at painting long enough.'

Rowena slowly left the door and walked back to
the desk where her father sat watching her with a
gleam of speculation in his small eyes. 'You promised!' she said in a hushed voice.

'Didn't exactly promise,' Gerald Southall replied
stoutly, now looking at a spot on the wall behind
Rowena's head and refusing to meet her eyes. 'Just
had second thoughts, that's all.'

'But you can't——' Rowena gasped then
stopped. 'He's already at the Slade, and you can't
alter that!' she added with a touch of triumph in
her voice.

'I can take his allowance away,' her father returned placidly, as if enjoying himself, and
Rowena was sure he was. 'Been thinking,' he went
on. 'Art's all right, but there's no guarantee he'll
ever make a living from it. He can always play at it
in his spare time. I've decided to put him in the
London office for a start,' he added, as he cast a
quick surreptitious glance at her.

'He won't go,' Rowena replied steadily. 'You
know he won't.' She stared at the rich carpeted
floor of the study as she tried to come to terms
with her father's latest bombshell. 'He can apply
for a grant.'

'And just how much do you think he'll get?'
queried Gerald Southall loftily. 'Certainly not
enough to keep him in that nice Chelsea apartment
with the studio in the roof. No. He'll have to take
up some sort of work—such as waiting at table in
one of those large restaurants—or washing-up till

all hours of night. That's what other students do. They haven't their fathers' wallets to cushion them. No, my mind's made up. In years to come he'll thank me for looking out for his future.'

Rowena was still picturing David at the sink in one of those large restaurants her father had mentioned, with piles of dirty plates stacked up beside him—and not only that, she closed her eyes, the fact that he would have to look for lodgings, and goodness knows they were hard enough to find. As for food—she shuddered. He wouldn't bother about a small thing like that. He'd be too tired for a start, she thought miserably, working half the night to make ends meet. Her eyes opened and rested on her father and there was something in his expression that alerted her to his thoughts, and she suddenly saw that she had been a long time getting there. She swallowed. 'If I agree to what——' she couldn't finish, and started again. 'You know what I'm talking about. Well, if I do, I want your promise that you'll leave David alone, and keep on with his allowance.' Her eyes glinted as she saw him nod slowly. 'I mean it, Father,' she said quietly. 'No going back on your word this time. Whatever happens, you'll leave David alone. If you go back on your word, then I'll leave you and join David— between us we can earn enough to keep him on at the Slade. I want nothing else but to see him where he belongs.'

Her father had not liked that ultimatum at all, but merely inclined his head. 'You have my word,' he said huffily. 'I don't recall giving you that before, and I've never gone back on my word.'

'Whatever happens,' Rowena insisted. 'I want your word on that, too.'

'Whatever happens,' repeated Gerald Southall, showing signs of losing his temper. 'Now I've a few calls to make.'

As Rowena left the study, she was in no doubt as to who would be the recipient of the first call, and couldn't help feeling a little spiteful gratification that she wouldn't be the only one to receive a shock that morning. Sean Tancred was in for a similar jolt, and unless she was very much mistaken, so was her father, as she envisaged Sean Tancred's reaction to her father's proposal. She had hardly spoken to the man, but she had watched him constantly when he had been present at the few social occasions she had attended and had gained the impression that he was a very forthright man, quite apart from being the handsomest man she had ever seen. His height and white-blond hair would have commanded attention anywhere, but his personality was such that he would have automatically have been the centre of any gathering even without his claim of lineal birth in a family that could be traced back in the Domesday Book.

These thoughts had automatically led her back to a comment of her father's a short while ago, of how she had thrown 'moony' looks Sean Tancred's way, and a deep flush suffused her pale features. With her mother, she had made periodic visits to the village since she was eleven years old, and had spent the odd weekend there with Jenny Heysham. The visits had been of too short a duration for the children to have formed any attachments to the village children, but there had been one occasion when Rowena had attended a dance given at Tancred House to raise funds for a school outing, and Miss Heysham in her capacity as headmistress had been detailed to organise the affair, and had taken her old college friend Julia Southall and her daughter with her.

Rowena moved restlessly away from the window as if to thrust these unhappy thoughts away from her, but they persisted and would not let her be. She had been just seventeen then, she recalled, and had worn her first long party dress. Her large brown eyes fastened unseeingly on the wall opposite her; even now she could still feel the excitement of that occasion. To actually be going to Tancred House, where she could be absolutely certain of seeing the man who had filled her thoughts since she was twelve years old and had attended a prize-giving ceremony at the village school where her mother had been detailed to help with the refreshments, as most of the usual helpers had not unnaturally wanted to watch their various offspring receive whatever honours they had achieved during the year.

It had been the first time that Rowena had seen Sean Tancred, for he had presented the prizes, and she didn't remember anything else about that occasion. The tall fair young man had haunted her dreams from then on, and to her he was the Knight of Knight's Gate.

This youthful 'crush' that she had had on him had lasted through the years, and she would be in a fever of impatience for her mother's next visit to the village, and used to dream of being asked to stay with Miss Heysham throughout the summer holidays, but the dream was never realised, for her father would always arrange a long holiday for them in some other part of the world, and Rowena had had to be content with the spasmodic visits during the year.

As it was only a small village, it was a very close-knit community, and an extremely active one. Cricket matches were held each Sunday on the village green in the true village tradition during the summer months, and various other activities pursued throughout the year. It had not taken the lovelorn Rowena long to find out that her 'Knight' was captain of the local eleven, and with David in tow she would slip out of Miss Heysham's cottage on the edge of the green and watch the match. David had been a willing partaker in this move; boylike, he had been only too pleased to absent himself from the interminable gossip of his mother and Miss Heysham, who never seemed to run out of conversation, and anything was better than that.

Rowena would stand as near as she dared to the circle of friends who always hung about Sean Tancred, and would listen shamelessly to the conversation just to hear the smooth intonation of his voice as he joked with them.

It had never occurred to her that such constant hovering on the edge of the crowd would attract much notice, for she was very careful to keep in the background of such gatherings, but she had not taken into account the fact that she was a stranger to the villagers, even though they knew who she was, and that she had visited the village on and off for the past few years. She was not of the village and therefore a stranger, and as such would automatically arouse their interest.

None of this had she known until the night of the dance at Tancred House. Her hands clenched themselves into small fists as she made herself go over the evening that had been the worst evening in her young life.

To the expectant Rowena, the evening was set for a fairytale ending. Not that she dared to hope that her hero would ask her to dance with him, that would be too much to expect, but she would actually see where he lived, really see it, not just the huge old building that overlooked the village and was more in the nature of a castle than a house. Her mother, she recalled, had been just as anxious to see inside the fine old house as she had, but for a different reason, for she remembered her remarking to Miss Heysham one day that the house should be opened to the public because of its historical interest, and Miss Heysham had replied that that had been a wish of Mr Tancred's, but it would take a lot of money to put it in order before such a thing could happen, and it was all he could do to keep the estate intact fighting the rising cost of management.

All this went through Rowena's mind as a sort of prelude to the misery she was later to suffer, but she made herself go on.

The house was even larger than it appeared from the outside. She remembered a huge hall, with a fireplace large enough to hold uncut lengths of wood, two long, heavy lances crossed on the wall above the fireplace, and above them an ancient coat of arms. Rowena experienced once again the thrill she had felt on seeing those lances. It was truly a knight's castle, and as she passed a suit of armour at the top of the wide oak staircase on the way to the cloakrooms to deposit their coats, Rowena's cup of happiness was filled as she imagined her knight wearing that suit of armour.

She could clearly remember everything that evening until she had overheard some chance remarks from two girls who had been in the cloakroom when she had made a visit halfway through the evening.

For the convenience of the guests, a small suite in the west wing of the house had been allocated for this purpose, and Rowena, hearing voices in the adjoining bathroom, had waited in the bedroom, using the time to tidy up her appearance. She could recall thinking how handsome her knight had looked that evening. She had never seen him in evening dress before, and her heart had raced at the thought that perhaps he might ask her to dance, but so far he had seemed totally unaware of her presence in the huge ballroom, and she had been forced to adopt the old gambit of hanging around the fringe of his friends in order to catch a sight of him.

She swallowed. How foolish she had been in thinking that her actions would pass unnoticed in such a crowd. If she had only known—She took a deep breath. How cruel people could be, she thought sadly. She had been living in a world of fantasy that concerned no one but herself—or so she had thought, until she had heard one of the girls tell the other to hurry up. 'We don't want to leave Sean too long or he might get landed with that Southall girl. She was on watch duty again tonight, I noticed, and Sean would never forgive us for deserting him in his hour of need,' she had added with a chuckle.

Her companion had also laughed. 'I won't be a minute, but this wretched hair of mine won't lie flat,' she had commented. 'It's a good job that girl's family doesn't live here. Just imagine poor Sean's embarrassment if she was around all the time! I think he's seriously considering asking Miss Heysham to either move or to fall out with her bosom friend,' she said dryly.

'Oh, Di, he isn't! Is he?' queried the other girl with a trace of amusement in her voice.

'Of course not!' replied Di exasperatedly, 'but I think he's getting fed up with falling over her everywhere he goes—said she reminds him of a spaniel they once had. It used to stand by its food bowl and look at him just the way she does.'

A howl of laughter had greeted this statement, and the stunned Rowena was galvanised into action and flung herself out of the bedroom before the girls emerged upon her, and had spent the rest of that evening sitting by her mother's side in one of the anterooms off the ballroom chatting to Miss Heysham, and strongly resisting any of their attempts to send her back to the ballroom.

Her soft mouth twisted at the memory. That had been five years ago, and during those years she had managed to avoid visiting Knight's Gate again. If their usually quiet daughter had appeared even quieter to her parents, not much notice was taken of this, and as her mother was taken ill a few months after their return to London, everything else had paled into insignificance. After her mother's death, it was no hard task to refuse the standing invitation to visit Miss Heysham, and although Rowena felt guilty at deserting her mother's friend, she compensated for this by sending her chatty letters from time to time.

It had been a blow when her father had decided to settle in the place where she had had such an unhappy experience, but nothing Rowena could say would change his mind.

Until a short while ago, she had been unaware that her father knew of her youthful crush on Sean Tancred, but he did not know of the humiliation she had suffered in respect of this. For this she was devoutly grateful, otherwise she might have suspected him of choosing this method of getting his own back on the proud village squire who had likened his daughter to a pet spaniel of his. All this Rowena had kept deep within her bruised emotions, and it had haunted her thoughts and made her even shyer in the company of the male of the species—shy and very unsure of herself. Only in her capacity of secretary and hostess for her father at the numerous sherry parties or dinner parties her father would hold from time to time did she feel safe, as these were business gatherings and she could talk to her father's business compatriots in their own language and was accepted not as a divertive ornament but as a useful aide to her father's business.

So they had come to Knight's Gate, and now lived in a fine house on the outskirts of the village. That had been six months ago, and during that time Rowena had studiously avoided any contact with the village functions, especially any occasions which Sean Tancred might be expected to attend, and that included most of them, since he took a great interest in the village social life, as had his father before him, for these were in a sense his people, and all had worked on the estate at one time or another, the various duties passing down from father to son through the centuries.

Strangely enough, Rowena was not lonely. She was never tired of the changing scenes of nature, and when her secretarial duties allowed she would take long walks through the woods that lay at the back of her new home accompanied by Goldie, her labrador, who was now just coming out of the puppy stage and had proved a lovable companion for her in her constant rambles.

It was through Miss Heysham that Rowena had heard all the local gossip, the most surprising being that Sean Tancred was still a bachelor, for she had felt certain that he would be married by then, but married or not, Rowena would never be able to forget the past, and had dreaded finding herself anywhere in his vicinity. She couldn't have hoped to be utterly successful in this, since it was a small village, but apart from an embarrassing meeting one morning when she had called upon Miss Heysham to find him installed in her sitting room drinking the cup of coffee that Miss Heysham had insisted on giving him during a discussion on school affairs she had not seen him. On Rowena's arrival he had seemed just as startled to see her as she was to see him, and had taken his departure soon afterwards.

For how long this state of affairs could have gone on, Rowena had no idea, but she had a vague hope that her father would weary of the country life and suggest that they move elsewhere, preferably somewhere not too far out of town but with country combined, as Rowena would miss her walks with Goldie.

But for the fact that he had still kept up with his various business interests, although he had retired from active dealings in the city, Rowena was sure that they would have made the move back to what he might once have described as 'civilisation' long before now, and it was really only his pugnacious nature that had made him refuse to be beaten.

Fawned upon and looked up to in the City because of his business acumen that had accumulated him a great deal of money as he was, it had come as a shock to find himself kept on the fringe of the local gentry, and worse than that, made to stand in line with the lesser lights of the village waiting for membership to the village golf club—a membership that would automatically bring him into constant contact with the village hierarchy, who might not be wealthy, but like the Tancred family, had lived in the locality for almost as long as the squire had, although as with the squire's family, their fortunes had dwindled with the passage of time, but their pride had remained intact.

Rowena stirred restlessly. Going over the past was not going to help her now. It only made further nonsense of what had happened, and she still could not believe that Sean Tancred had accepted her father's terms, in spite of the bald fact that less than an hour ago he had stood in the room she was now in and calmly told her that he would stand by the terms outlined by her father in return for his monetary help in righting the affairs of his estate.

As she went over that short but highly embarrassing interlude, she had to revise her earlier
thoughts. Hardly calmly, she thought. In fact Sean
had been absolutely furious at finding himself in
such a position, and his scathing, 'Was it your
idea?' had left her little room for pride.

Her slim hands clenched together. He had made
no bones about his feelings in the matter. He had
simply refused to even consider the fact that she
was as stunned by his acceptance of her father's
offer as he must have been when it was first put to
him. On recalling what her father had said about
grandchildren, she gave an hysterical chuckle.
Only someone as insensitive as her father could
have made a remark like that at that time.

She got up abruptly. It simply would not do.
Things had gone far enough. She gave a slight
shudder as she envisaged the future as pointed out
to her by the autocratic man her father had chosen
as her husband, and her eyes went to David's
painting. 'I'm sorry, David, but I can't do it,' she
whispered. 'I can't pay that price, and you
wouldn't want me to.'

CHAPTER TWO

ROWENA spent the rest of that morning working
out ways and means of extricating herself from the
impossible situation she had found herself in
through no fault of her own.

She had considered ringing up Sean Tancred and telling him that she had had second thoughts on the matter and would he please forget the whole wretched scheme, and adding something on the lines that she had only agreed to the plan in the certainty that he would refuse to go along with her father's conditions for the financial help he was offering. Rowena would have enjoyed adding that rider. It would have been some consolation for the embarrassment she had been subjected to in his presence earlier that day.

Further thought on these lines, however, made her hastily reject this plan. Not only would she enrage the proud squire of Knight's Gate, but also her father, who would be bound to think up some horribly devious way of getting back at her through David, and who could reasonably argue that as she had gone back on her word, he had no hesitation in going back on his.

As she could find no inspiration in the confines of the house, Rowena decided to take Goldie for a walk through the woods in the hope that the soft country air might clear her thinking and give her a brainwave as to how to cope with this crisis that had suddenly been thrust upon her.

April, she thought as she strode through the woods just showing signs of new life, was the loveliest time of the year, and certainly not the time to contemplate going back to the grime of the city, but if all else failed that was just what she would have to do. How she was going to cope with Goldie in whatever lodgings she managed to find with David was something she would rather not think about at that time. Not while watching her chasing a blackbird who had flown to a nearby tree for safety at Goldie's enthusiastic approach to a moving object.

It was not as if she could leave Goldie to her father's tender care. He did not particularly care for animals. There was Miss Heysham, of course, but Rowena did not think she could place such an obligation on her. If she had wanted a dog she would have got herself one by now, and an animal of Goldie's size needed plenty of exercise, and it wouldn't be fair of Rowena to even hint at such an arrangement.

Rowena looked ahead of her, and high on the hill beyond the wood sat the home her father had chosen for her in his quest for acceptance into the realms of the gentry. Her eyes narrowed against a shaft of sunlight that suddenly pierced through the glade in which she was standing. It had always looked a proud dwelling, as proud as its owner, but there had been nothing forbidding in its old walled structure before. Now it seemed to leer back at her, making her feel precisely what she was, an intruder, buying her way into the aristocracy. She gave a slight shudder and looked away from Tancred House, wondering how she could ever have once had romantic dreams about such a place, or its owner, come to that, she thought ironically. It just went to show how very naïve she had been when she was seventeen. The village girls had been light years ahead of her all the way.

Her brow creased in thought as she continued on her way. There must be some way in which she could back out of the mess her father had landed her in. It was no use going to him and relying on his sympathy to get her out of the proposition. He would only repeat what he had said before, that she would come to accept it. Unless she was very mistaken, he was already planning to hold a big engagement party for her, and her soft lips twisted at the thought of Sean Tancred's reaction to such a gathering.

On recalling his harsh words about not bothering to utter the conventional words, she doubted if he would be prepared to play along with such blatant tactics, and was sure that he would refuse point blank. Her father had a lot to learn in that direction, she thought shrewdly, and it wouldn't be long before he found out that money couldn't buy everything, and certainly not a man like Sean Tancred.

Rowena sighed. She had been sure that he would refuse her father's offer, but he had accepted it, and she was still finding that hard to believe. It had come as a shock to him, of course. He could have had no idea what her father had wanted to see him about that morning, and knowing her father, Rowena guessed that he hadn't bothered to wrap it up, but had thrown it at him in no uncertain way.

Her eyes suddenly opened wide. That must be it! Shock did produce odd results that could be completely out of character with one's normal behaviour.

Sean Tancred was fighting a losing battle against the rising cost of living. He had been fighting it all that time ago when Rowena used to visit Knight's Gate with her mother. It was a load he had had to carry on his broad shoulders ever since he had inherited his father's estate, probably when still in his late teens.

How would such a man react to a pot of gold being dangled in front of him? Precisely as he had reacted, she thought sagely. At that time it would have appeared too good a chance to miss, but afterwards, when he had had time to think about things—such as acquiring an unwanted bride in the bargain—surely then—— She swallowed. All her father wanted was an entrée into high society, and with a little deviousness surely this could be accomplished without the misery of an unwanted marriage.

Rowena's steps quickened in her excitement. It ought to work. All she had to do was to get Sean Tancred's co-operation, and that shouldn't be hard, considering that he must already be having second thoughts on the matter.

Goldie had to be called twice. She didn't like having her walk cut short so early, but eventually she pounded back to Rowena's side as she turned towards home.

To Rowena's relief her father elected to take lunch in his study, leaving her in solitary peace in the dining room. Her mind was full of the plan she had conceived during her walk, and which just needed a little polishing and the right way to present it to Sean Tancred.

Of course, he would not like the idea of her father taking an active part in the running of the estate, but as unpopular as her father was among his past employees, his methods got results, and results produced income. There was also no doubt that given the opportunity, Gerald Southall would jump at the chance offered. If what Rowena had heard about Sean Tancred's hopes of opening Tancred House to the public after the necessary renovations had been carried out, then she could think of no better an administrator than her father to watch over this work—or better still, she thought happily, the appointment of estate manager! When it came to business matters, her father undoubtedly had the Midas touch.

Once she had produced what she was certain was a foolproof plan that would be acceptable to all parties, all that remained to be done was to carry it out—well, for Sean Tancred to carry it out, for the initiative would have to come from him, it could hardly come from her. It would be he that would have to contact her father on the grounds that he wanted another discussion with him, and that would be perfectly natural under the circumstances. During that discussion he would only have to suggest an alternative to the scheme suggested earlier and dangle another proposition before him. It would not be a difficult task for a clever man, and Rowena was certain that Sean Tancred was a match for her father any day. A little flattery would work wonders, she was sure, something on the lines of astute business sense being required to put the estate in order.

It might be as well, she told herself with a frown, if he made it quite clear right from the start of the discussion that he had no intention of marrying her. He could rightly claim that he had not been given enough time to make a decision on such an important issue, and then propose the alternative, otherwise he might find himself landed not only with an unwanted bride, but with her father as well, and that was more than could be asked of any man. Not that Rowena could see Sean Tancred making such a lamentable error, no matter how much financial help he required.

When she heard her father retire to his room after lunch to take the nap his doctor had insisted upon his doing, Rowena ran up to her own room and snatching up a light cardigan, dashed down the stairs again and out of the front door before Goldie, who would be playing in the kitchen garden at the back of the house, knew that she had gone out.

There was not a moment to be wasted. With any luck Sean Tancred would be making an appointment to see her father that evening, thus nipping in the bud any plans he might have been making in connection with the marriage he had hoped to promote.

The sense of urgency carried her down the drive of her home and through the village and up the hill towards the long driveway that led to Tancred House. It made her impervious to anything but her goal, and it seemed an anticlimax when she at last reached the huge studded ancient doors of the house and pulled at the equally ancient-looking bell knob at the side of the door.

'I'd like to see Mr Tancred,' she announced breathlessly to the elderly woman in a flowered printed overall who answered the door, and blinked in dismay as the woman said that the master was out 'on the estate somewhere,' but relented enough to suggest that Rowena try the old stables at the back of the house where she had an idea he might be located.

Rowena thanked her and asked her which way she ought to go to get to the stables, and the woman pointed to the left side of the house, and told her to carry on down that side until she came to some french windows, where there was a pathway just beyond the house that would eventually lead her to the stables.

It seemed a long way to the anxious Rowena, but eventually she came to some old low-lying buildings badly needing urgent repairs and what must be the stabling area. As she approached the double doors of the first building she came to, her heart was thudding, not only through her hurried approach to Tancred House, but the urgency of her mission.

As soon as she reached the doors she knew that there was someone in the stable. She could hear the metallic clink of what sounded like tackle being moved, and called out a timid, 'Hallo!'

A second later Sean Tancred came into view, and as he saw his visitor, Rowena saw his firm lips straighten in a line of annoyance as he walked towards her from the dark recesses of the stable where he had obviously been working. His usually immaculate white shirt was rolled up to his elbows and the collar was open at the neck. His dun-coloured corduroys had certainly seen better days, but for all that he still presented a force to be reckoned with in anybody's book. 'Well!' he growled at the now timid Rowena, who was beginning to have second thoughts on her good idea. He couldn't even bring himself to give her a civil welcome. 'Come to look over your property, have you?' he sneered. 'Couldn't wait, was that it? Well, I'm afraid you're going to have to. It hasn't hap-

pened yet,' he added harshly, 'and until then, I'd
be obliged if you'd keep your distance.'

Rowena felt as if he had taken a whip to her.
Her eyes widened at his implication that she was
insensitive enough to thrust herself upon his
domain without invitation. As to 'looking over her
property'—she swallowed. What a hateful man he
was, and to think she was trying to help him! 'I
didn't come for that,' she managed to get out, surprised how calm her voice sounded in spite of the
fury she could feel building up inside her. 'I want
to talk to you.'

His blue gaze swept disdainfully over her slim
figure with her dark hair now windswept, like a
dark cloud framing her pale features. She hadn't
bothered about her appearance, but now she
wished she had, and a slight flush mounted her
cheeks as she suffered his grim appraisal. He
folded his arms across his chest, and she was very
conscious of the thick cluster of fine golden hair
along those strong arms of his. 'Well, talk away,'
he growled, 'only don't drag it out. I've some
work to do.'

Rowena's previous plans for gaining his co-
operation in defeating her father's hopes for her
future were thrust aside by her fury, not to mention pride. So she and David would live in an attic
somewhere—anything was better than having to
suffer this detestable man's company. She only
knew she wanted to get back at him, hurt him as
he had hurt her, not only in his attitude now, but
for the unhappiness she had suffered in the past. 'I
want you to ask me to marry you,' she found herself saying loudly but firmly.

She knew a feeling of malicious triumph at the way Sean's blue eyes registered the shock she had given him, then they narrowed. 'Want your money's worth, do you?' he asked pithily.

Rowena nodded, too angry to regret her impulsiveness.

'Very well, if you insist,' he drawled insolently. 'Will you do me the honour of becoming my wife, Miss Southall?' He swept her a bow that like the tone of his words told of his dislike of the situation, and this pleased her too.

'My name is Rowena,' she replied sweetly. 'I think it would sound better if you used it, and also if you added "please".'

Sean's face hardened and Rowena almost took a step backward at the fury in his eyes as he stared back at her. 'I don't think I'm that hard up,' he grated out harshly. 'You can tell your father that I've changed my mind. Now I'd be obliged if you'd get the hell out of here.'

Rowena felt a surge of pure relief flow through her heightened emotions. It was as if she had been holding her breath all day waiting for just such a happening, and now she felt lightheaded.

It was all she could do not to show her elation. Her father would keep his promise and not make life difficult for David—not unless he got to hear of her visit to Tancred House. 'I think you ought to tell him yourself,' she said quietly, hoping that the anxiety she was beginning to feel did not show in her voice.

'Afraid of him, are you?' Sean sneered, then gave a grim nod. 'Come to think of it, it will be a pleasure,' he added, as he strode out of the stables and walked towards the next building.

Just before he went into the building Rowena called out hastily, 'I'd rather you didn't tell him that I've been to see you.'

As he did not answer, she was forced to follow him into the building. It was a stores area, and at the end of the room was a makeshift office. Rowena's anxious eyes watched him go to the desk and pick up the receiver and start to dial her number. 'I don't want him to know I'm here,' she repeated firmly, but some of the panic she felt inevitably reached the man holding the receiver, and he paused in the dialling action and turned towards her.

'Just where do you stand in all this?' he demanded, then his autocratic brows rose as a thought occurred to him. 'Don't tell me you didn't know what he was up to?' he queried.

Rowena felt her cheeks flame under his hard scrutiny and looked away quickly from those very blue eyes that saw too much for her liking. 'Only a short while before you did,' she replied in a low voice, fixing her gaze on a pile of crates stacked in a corner opposite her.

'And you agreed?' he persisted harshly.

She swallowed. She still couldn't look at him, and gave a small nod. 'Only because——' she faltered here, but made herself go on, thinking miserably that nothing was going according to plan, and she needn't have bothered, 'because I was sure you would have nothing to do with it,' she ended lamely.

'And I let you down, is that it?' he shot out at her. Another thought then hit him and he gave her a piercing stare. 'What the devil was that about, then?' he growled, referring to their previous conversation, and the one question that she would have preferred not to have replied to.

Her brown eyes met his steadily as she answered, 'It was the only way I could think of to make you change your mind.'

She watched his eyes widen as he got the implication behind her words. 'And you were going to turn me down, was that the way of it?' he asked softly, in a tone that Rowena didn't much care for as she could imagine how that would infuriate him.

She took a deep breath. 'Yes,' she answered, tossing her head in a defiant action. Now it was out she had no need to apologise. It was about time he realised a few home truths.

Sean stood looking down at her for what seemed an age to the inwardly quaking Rowena, then pointed a long aristocratic finger towards a rickety-looking chair beside the desk, indicating that she should be seated. 'I'd like to hear more,' he said, still in that soft voice, 'such as why you agreed to the scheme in the first place.'

'I can't stop,' Rowena said quickly, the panic now plainly visible in her voice. 'It's almost time for tea, and Father will want to know where I am, if I'm not there to take it with him.'

'Very well,' Sean replied casually, and picked up the receiver again and began dialling. 'One way or the other, I intend to get to the bottom of this. I'm sure your father will be more accommodating.'

'Please don't ring him!' Rowena pleaded, and went to the chair and sat down. 'I suppose I could stay a little longer.'

The silence was oppressive as she sat trying to sort out her thoughts. No matter how she explained it, it wouldn't look good, and she jumped when Sean growled, 'Well?'

Her fingers played along the edge of the chair in her agitation, then she took a deep breath. 'As I told you. I knew nothing of what he had in mind until this morning. He just threw it at me,' she said, her voice unknowingly echoing the shock she had received. She swallowed. 'I didn't believe—I couldn't really believe he would go ahead with it——' her fingers moved along the edge of the chair again. 'I asked him not to go ahead,' she added in a low voice, 'but he wouldn't listen—and there were reasons why I had to agree to do what he wanted——' She stopped, suddenly realising that she had already said more than she should have done.

'What reasons?' Sean asked harshly.

Rowena's fingers clenched hard on the chair. Why had he to know that? she wondered crossly. It was nothing to do with him. She licked her dry lips. He was waiting for an answer and she had to think of something, apart from the truth. He would only laugh at the thought of David losing his allowance. He wouldn't understand any of it. She took a deep breath. 'There was something I wanted,' she said quietly. 'It was a sort of bargain I made with him.' She looked up at him quickly. 'It was nothing to do with you,' she added hastily, 'just something I wanted his promise on.'

Far from proving a satisfactory explanation her reply infuriated him, that she could see by the har-

dened expression on his face and the derisory look
in his eyes as he looked at her. 'A bigger allowance—or a fur coat, I presume,' he said with heavy
sarcasm. 'A sort of tails you lose, heads I win
basis,' he sneered.

Rowena flushed. He could say what he liked,
she thought furiously, it didn't matter to her, just
as long as she could extricate herself from the jam
she was in. 'As a matter of fact, yes,' she replied
spiritedly, and got up from the chair. She had said
all that she was going to say and now wanted to
put as much distance between them as was possible. She fervently hoped she would never see him
again. 'Don't bother to ring Father,' she said airily
as she reached the door. 'I'll convey your message
to him.'

'What message?' Sean asked blandly, making
her come to an abrupt halt at the door and turn
round to face him.

'You know very well what message,' Rowena
replied furiously. 'That you've changed your
mind—what else?'

'And lose my golden bride?' he said softly. 'Oh,
no. I've revised that decision. You see,' he went on
blandly, 'I have two options left open to me.
Before your father so gallantly came to my rescue,
I only had one way out of my difficulties. That
was to sell off part of my land to an aspiring
building consortium that would have put up rows
of little red boxes that they amusingly call houses.'
His strong hands clenched into businesslike-look-
ing fists as he said this, 'and within a few years I
should have found myself in the middle of a vast
housing complex.' His grim eyes met Rowena's

startled ones. 'That was the reason why I chose to accept the offer.' He gave an offhand shrug. 'Beggars can't be choosers, Miss Southall.'

Rowena wished she had not left her chair, for her knees felt decidedly weak as she slowly grasped what he was saying. 'You mean——?' she said in a voice of disbelief.

He gave a curt nod, and suddenly smiled at her, and the smile was not a pleasant one. 'The agreement stands,' he grated, 'and I wouldn't advise you to break it. Your father had the foresight to have the whole agreement in writing. If you back out, then I shall sue your father for every penny he owns—in fact,' he nodded savagely, 'I believe I should really enjoy that.' He gave her another smile, no less pleasant than the other one. 'You know, you really ought to be more careful where you place your bets. This horse has definitely entered the race.' He gave a cursory glance at his wrist watch. 'And now, Miss Southall, if you would care for a guided tour over the property I can spare you another half-hour.'

Rowena could only remember dully shaking her head wordlessly before she made her escape. If she had been in a state of apprehension when she had arrived at Tancred House, the result of her call had hardly helped to relieve it. She never remembered reaching home. All her movements seemed automatic, and so was her response to her father when he told her that evening that the wedding date had been fixed. It was to be precisely a fortnight from that date.

'Tancred knows what he wants,' he had remarked in a satisfied voice. 'I like a man who doesn't quibble over things.' He looked at the silent Rowena. 'He suggested that you call in one day and have a word with the housekeeper, a Mrs Broom, or something like that, about the reception,' he gave a low chuckle. 'Got a move on, didn't he? If he's as quick in getting me into that hallowed club of theirs, I've nothing to complain about,' he ended happily.

Rowena went to bed early that night. She was not only tired but mentally exhausted. Her brain had gone round in circles since her visit to Tancred House, and she was still finding it hard to believe that she was actually going to marry Sean Tancred. If she was having a nightmare and had dreamed the whole thing up, then it was a long nightmare, and she was very much afraid that it was going to last a lifetime.

CHAPTER THREE

THE engagement party that Rowena had surmised that her father would arrange took place a week later, and like everything else that had happened to her since her father's shattering announcement, it passed like a scene in a play to the utterly bemused Rowena.

It did not take much imagination on her part to realise that her life of quiet but contented obscurity had vanished beyond recall. As Sean Tancred's wife she could not hope to remain in the background, in spite of his hard comments on her status. That had been for her ears alone, and she was sure that few of the villagers would be aware of the true state of the marriage.

Had she allowed her imagination any further rein, she would have taken to her heels, since just the thought of living in close proximity with such a man as Sean Tancred gave her palpitations, but like the pealing bell of doom, his hard voice would come through to her, if she backed out, he would ruin her father, and she had no doubt on this score. As he had said, he would relish such a chance. He liked her father no better than he liked her. In his opinion they were pushing social climbers with more money than breeding, who thought they could buy their way into high society. Where her father was concerned he was perfectly correct, Rowena had to concede, but now she was tainted with the same brush and it was all so unfair.

When her father had told her of the party he was throwing to celebrate her engagement, Rowena said nothing, but her immediate reaction was that Sean Tancred would have nothing to do with it, and she couldn't see how her father could expect him to. To actually say so would be a waste of breath and she was beyond any arguments. It was as if she was being carried along by a swift unrelenting tide of events from which she was powerless to escape and could only hope for some kind of miracle that would alter the course of events.

To add to her confused state of mind, Sean Tancred actually attended the engagement party. Knowing her father, it wouldn't have surprised her if he had carried on with his plans if he hadn't;

he was so determined to pass on the news of what he considered his daughter's good fortune in obtaining such a match, and wouldn't have been a bit put out by the non-appearance of the intended groom.

All in all it was a series of letdowns for Rowena, who now felt that no one could be relied upon. She would have confidently predicted that Sean would not attend the party, yet here he was, by all accounts having no objection to the gathering, and receiving the congratulations of his friends after the announcement had been made.

While Rowena received similar congratulations, and kept moving among the guests to prevent the embarrassment of having to stand beside the man she was destined to marry, it occurred to her that the only person who had been right in his summing-up of his future son-in-law had been her father. He had accurately judged his man. His estate came first, and even his stiff pride had had to bow to this.

It also occurred to her that she had made a bad mistake in going to see him that day, when she had hoped to get his co-operation in foiling her father's plans for her future. Through no fault of her own, her scheme had backfired on her. From Sean Tancred's point of view it had been a disastrous step to take, and just another thorn to add to his already outraged dignity. To have to marry a woman he had no liking for was bad enough, but to find that same woman using him as a counter in a gamble to obtain something she wanted was enough to guarantee a stormy passage ahead for such an unwise person.

This was not just surmising on Rowena's part, it was a bald fact. She could expect no sympathy or understanding from that quarter. It was in Sean's cold eyes whenever they rested upon her that evening, in spite of his over-studied politeness to her in company whenever they were forced to pair up to receive congratulations.

Remembering his hard words on her future status, Rowena could only be thankful for small mercies. He had wanted her to stay out of his life and she was only too pleased to accommodate this wish. Anything else would be sheer misery for both of them.

Had she not been so engrossed with her own inward misery, she might have found time to wonder at the way the villagers took the news in their stride and rallied around their squire, as if this sort of arrangement was common practice, and willing to accept an outsider as his lady, for there could be no misunderstanding as to why such an arrangement had been made.

This state of affairs should have made Rowena feel less embarrassed and able to cope with the obnoxious position she had been placed in, but even when such thoughts did sink through the haze of unhappiness surrounding her, it made little difference. She still felt like a walking gift-wrapped bonus, and should have had a tag somewhere on her person that stated how much she was worth to the man she was marrying.

The fact that she had, at one time or another, made some acquaintance with the local guests, even if it was only a smile in passing in the village street, somewhat eased the situation for her, but it could not ease the ache in her heart. There were a few of her father's business acquaintances too, and whenever she found the going hard, she would gravitate towards that group, for these were the people she felt she had more in common with, and once the teasing and sincere wishes for her future were over with, she was able to relax until a local dignitary claimed her attention.

It was not hard to see why the villagers, particularly the older ones, had accepted the situation with such bonhomie. To them such a marriage was plain common sense, and they appeared to the bitter Rowena to be applauding their squire's astute choice of partner, and she wondered just how much the village had progressed down the years and came to the conclusion that while time had marched on, this sleepy hamlet still retained the old-world ideals where property was concerned.

In spite of her bitterness Rowena could understand their way of thinking. Sean Tancred's terse comments on the options left open to him as a way out of his financial dilemma had given her an understanding of how bad things were. His plans for the opening of Tancred House to the public would invariably bring trade to the village, and as portly Colonel Fisher had jovially put it, 'place the village on the map'. There was also the salient fact that not one of the residents had been in favour of being swallowed up by the ever-greedy development companies and eventually finding themselves on the edge of a new town.

With this thought in mind, it was easy to see why they had stood solidly behind Sean Tancred in his bid to solve his problems, and should have made Rowena feel more like the saviour of the village way of life than the 'golden bride' Sean had so tauntingly dubbed her that day.

Only in the younger generation did Rowena sense hostility, and this was to be expected, particularly from the females. During the course of the evening she had caught several open stares from two girls who had accompanied their parents to the party. One was Diana Fisher, daughter of Colonel Fisher, whose wife Melanie was a leading light in the village social affairs, and the other, obviously a close friend of Diana's, was Lucinda Dean, whose parents lived at the old Manor House, a rambling oak-structured building as old as Tancred House itself, and whose owners, Rowena heard from Miss Heysham, had served with the Tancred family since the days of Cromwell—a Charles Dean then serving under the Duke on the side of the Royalists.

Diana and Lucinda were in their middle twenties, Rowena guessed, and she was sure that they had been the girls she had unwittingly overheard talking in the cloakroom the evening she had visited Tancred House.

Diana Fisher was a tall, elegant blonde, with more than her fair share of beauty. Her natural blonde hair hung loose to her slim shoulders, and her finely boned features and greeny-blue eyes put one in mind of a woodland nymph. The filmy green dress that she wore, that floated round her slight figure rather than clothed it, enhanced this illusion and invariably conjured up another to the observant Rowena. In fairy stories of old, it would be just such a lovely creature that a gallant knight would fall in love with, and whom, after many trials and tribulations, he would eventually claim as his own.

These thoughts went through Rowena's mind as she watched Sean and Diana talking together that evening, and she wondered if they were in love, although there was nothing in Sean's behaviour to suggest such a state of affairs and she didn't know Diana well enough to gauge her feelings in the matter. Come to that, she didn't know Sean Tancred either, but they certainly made a lovely picture framed against the dark green velvet curtaining of the drawing-room windows.

While Rowena made small conversation with one of her father's business acquaintances, her eyes would invariably stray to that corner of the room. Sean's tall elegant figure, yet so very masculine, beside the frail blonde beauty of Diana, struck right at the heart of her unhappiness, glaringly exposing, to her way of thinking, the utter incredibility of the whole affair.

If anyone qualified as the potential squire's lady, then Diana Fisher would be first in line. She was absolutely perfect for the role, and as Rowena saw Sean's blond head bend to catch something Diana had said, her heart jerked painfully, not in jealousy but in sorrow, for surely these two belonged together. She would never belong to their world, she was a pushing outsider and would always be regarded as such, and it wasn't as if she hadn't tried to do something about it—she had, but had been ruthlessly prevented from backing out. Sean Tancred needed that money so badly he had been prepared to stand by her father's conditions, she thought bitterly. If he did love that slim beauty by his side, then he must be a very hard man indeed to go ahead with the arrangements, no matter how poor he was. Her one-time knight, she thought pithily, was turning out to be a black baron with a baron's worst attributes.

Rowena's depressed gaze then lingered on Lucinda Dean, who stood a little apart from her parents, and she was surprised to find herself undergoing a similar surreptitious scrutiny from Lucinda, who abruptly looked away as she caught Rowena's glance.

That one telling look practically confirmed Rowena's suspicions where Sean and Diana Fisher were concerned, for there was no doubt that Lucinda had taken an avid interest in Rowena as she had stood silent witness to Rowena's studied attention in that direction.

This depressed Rowena even further, and she wondered if Lucinda had more than a passing interest in the affair. Perhaps she was in love with the proud squire too, and it wouldn't have been at all surprising if she were. He had the looks and the bearing to enslave many hearts, and if Lucinda had become a casualty in the time-old game of love, then Rowena felt very sorry for her, for she felt they had much in common with each other, apart from the enslavement of the heart, because Rowena had long since been cured of that affliction. It was in nature's endowments, or rather the lack of them, that they were closely aligned, for neither was a beauty.

Lucinda's brown hair was a shade lighter than

Rowena's, normally termed 'mousey', a term Rowena would have applied to her own colouring, yet her hair was much darker and looked almost black against a light background, and unlike Lucinda's hung in loose short waves. Lucinda's would have looked much nicer if she had left it loose, Rowena thought, and not worn that bandeau to hold it back, and certainly not in that bright red colour that only served to emphasise her rather sallow complexion. The velvet dress she wore did nothing for her either, and in it she looked definitely uncomfortable, as if she would have felt more at home in a blouse and trews, as would Rowena if given the choice.

Rowena's dress of dove-grey velour was simple but expertly tailored. It looked just what it was, elegant and expensive; for Rowena's taste coincided with her father's in this respect and she knew exactly what suited her. Money had been no problem and the price only a secondary consideration, if she saw something that she liked.

As far as their figures were concerned, neither of them possessed any curves. It was straight up and down, but of the two of them Rowena came out on top, for her slight frame was neatly boyish, whereas Lucinda's was thin and bony.

Rowena sighed as she caught her father's admonishing eye that told her that she ought to be circulating among the guests and not standing looking lost in such a gathering, and she started on her rounds again, miserably contemplating that she couldn't hope to go on avoiding meeting up again with Sean, although so far she had managed to evade the embarrassment of having direct conversation with him, and when she had found herself beside him had been fortunate enough to find that he was engaged in conversation with one of the guests, and had been able to drift away without causing any untoward comment.

This time, however, she was dismayed to find herself standing near him with no one beside him, and as they were near the small bar that had been set up in the corner of the room, Rowena could only presume that he had been in the act of either replenishing his glass or Diana's, who, she noted, was now standing alone by the window and not showing any inclination to join the rest of the guests.

Her dismay soon turned to annoyance when she saw that Sean had no intention of rejoining Miss Fisher, and intended to stay put, even though he could have taken evasive action by casually strolling across the room to talk to one of his numerous friends, and gave her no option but to stay with him.

In tones of thinly disguised sarcasm he congratulated her on the success of the party and the distinguished gathering of City tycoons, a compliment that should have been directed at her father, since they were his friends, not Rowena's, but she knew that he would not believe her if she attempted to point this out to him, as she was sure that he was of the opinion that she was out to impress him with their rich influential friends.

While she politely listened to these double-edged compliments Rowena wished she could find some excuse to leave him, and as soon as there was a pause in the conversation she suggested that they circulate again, murmuring abstractedly that she thought Sir William Small, the property tycoon, looked as if he was waiting to have a word with him.

This plainly obvious attempt to remove herself from his presence only brought a silky warning to the effect that they would move when he was ready and not before, and an added taunt that she had only to announce her refusal to go ahead with the arrangement to bring an abrupt end to proceedings.

Infuriated, Rowena was sorely tempted to do just that, and for one rash moment she actually contemplated such an action, but one look at her father's satisfied, almost smug expression as he talked to Colonel Fisher brought her sharply down to earth. Not that she was all that fond of her father, but she did not hate him enough to do that to him. There was David to consider too, and his career was too important to her to throw it all away in a fit of temper. As for this hateful man standing by her side and watching her so closely, hoping that he had managed to goad her into making just such a mistake, she would have to disappoint him. Either way, she thought bitterly, he couldn't lose, and what was worse, he knew it. She forced herself to bestow a bright smile on him. 'I'm going to have to disappoint you,' she said in a low voice. 'You gave me no option, did you? I had hoped we could come to some other arrangement. That was the only reason why I came to see you that day.'

Sean's icy blue eyes clearly said that he didn't believe her, but his voice showed casual interest as he asked, 'What had you in mind, then, apart from the hope that I would act the grateful lover for monetary reasons?'

Rowena felt as if he had thrown a jug of cold water in her face, and her quick gasp of indignation was not lost on him. 'You're not going to believe me,' she managed to get out, 'but nothing would have been more distasteful to me if you'd attempted any such pose. I can well understand your reasoning,' she added pithily, 'you're so used to adulation, aren't you? It would simply never occur to you that you might be turned down, but just give me the chance,' she whispered vibrantly, 'and I'll prove it to you.' Her wide brown eyes met his challengingly. 'Drop out of the contract yourself. There are other ways—ways that I wanted to put to you until your aggressive attitude pushed them out of my mind.'

His narrowed eyes pierced hers. 'That was clever,' he said quietly, 'but not clever enough. As if you didn't know what would happen if I contracted out.' He took a deep breath as if seeking patience with her. 'To show you that I'm not the fool you apparently take me for I'll spell it out for you. Your father was well aware of such a possibility and made ample coverage. In other words, I forfeit the estate.' He gave a grim nod at Rowena's widening eyes as she comprehended this last bald statement. 'Oh yes, he did me the courtesy of making that quite plain to me before I signed the agreement. What he didn't foresee was your apparent reluctance to accept your part in the business.'

Rowena looked away quickly from those piercing eyes of his. She ought to have known that her father would have left nothing to chance, but she still felt ashamed at his forthright way of going about things.

'Do you know what I think?' Sean said silkily. 'I think you were well aware of this. I also think you put him up to it, but there were a few things that you didn't take into consideration. For one, you didn't expect me to see behind your smoke screen, and it must have come as a nasty shock to find that all you'd bought was a name and a lodging at Tancred House.' He gave an elegant shrug. 'No wonder you wanted to get back at me! All those romantic hopes of yours coming to nothing, after taking all that trouble only to find that I had no intention of playing the game your way. Even your father had the sense to realise that as much as I needed the money, there was a limit. As the old saying goes, you can lead a horse to water, but you can't make it drink.'

Rowena wanted to put her hands over her ears to shut out that hateful soft voice that was making her feel less than an inch high. It appeared their feelings were mutual. Sean disliked her as much as she disliked him, and she wanted to beg for some kind of truce that would release both of them from the impossible situation, but was powerless to utter a word in her defence.

His voice was now hard. 'As I've said, your father was sure of his ground where you were concerned. It never occurred to him that the same terms applied to him, and that he stood to lose a fortune if you backed out. So it's stalemate,' he added harshly, 'and now I suggest we circulate,'

and he strode away from the stunned Rowena,
who had to somehow force herself to act as if she
was enjoying herself in spite of the fact that she
felt that she was in the middle of a nightmare—
and how she could be expected to enjoy that was
beyond her comprehension.

CHAPTER FOUR

A WEEK later Rowena married Sean Tancred. The
ceremony took place in the centuries-old church in
the village, and was officiated over by the vicar.

Rowena had hoped that the ceremony would
take place at her home with a registrar in attendance, for under the circumstances the arrangement
hardly warranted a church blessing, but she was
forgetting Sean Tancred's position. As he was the
village squire such a ceremony would be expected,
even though the marriage was, to all intents and
purposes, a business arrangement.

At least Rowena was spared the necessity of
dressing up for the occasion in conventional white,
and wore a pale blue two-piece with a matching
picture hat.

In spite of the short time lapse between the engagement and the ceremony, Rowena felt as if
time had stood still. She did not know the person
who stood beside the tall elegant figure of Sean
Tancred in front of the ageing vicar of the parish,
and who duly repeated the marriage vows as if in a

trance and in a voice that was completely devoid of emotion.

During the reception held later in the huge ballroom of Tancred House, she maintained the same detached manner, and her too-bright smile that did not reach her eyes was good enough to fool all but those who really knew her. It would not have fooled David for one, but as he was away in the Highlands with no apparent locating address to inform him of the sudden turn of events, a matter that Rowena was profoundly grateful for, she was able to carry out her part without fear of discovery, although she had a few bad moments when Jenny Heysham determinedly tracked her down and expressed her surprise at the suddenness of the event, and had Rowena given herself time to think before irrevocably committing herself.

Not that she actually said this, but the carefully worded congratulations she gave her held such an anxiety, and Rowena recognised it and did her best to reassure her on this point. There was no doubt in Rowena's mind that she had heard the village gossip and had been dismayed by it on Rowena's account. At the time of the engagement she had been away visiting friends in Hertfordshire, and must have been amazed at the news on her return. Rowena had half expected her to call on her in order to ascertain the truth of the matter, and the fact that she had not done so told Rowena that she too had not forgotten the past and her adolescent crush on the handsome squire, a crush she was obviously convinced that Rowena still held and that was strong enough to propel her forward into what was surely a one-sided marriage.

Rowena had felt a little guilty at not going to see her before the wedding, but had made up for it by asking her to act as her attendant at the ceremony, taking the precaution of making her request on the telephone, that helpfully impersonal instrument that saved the necessity of confrontation, for Rowena was in no state to indulge in a cosy chat with anyone, let alone someone who had known her all those years—she dared not—for the need to confide her unhappiness to someone was too great a temptation and one she was sure to succumb to if given the chance, and there was too much at stake to allow herself this luxury.

Even at the reception, it seemed to Rowena that the separation made at the church of the bride's relations and friends on one side of the aisle and the groom's on the other remained the order of the day, for apart from the initial congratulations they drifted back into their own camps, the only exception being her father and herself, who where Rowena was concerned was forced to mingle with all and sundry, and where her father was concerned, determined to make his presence felt, intent on wringing the last ounce of triumph out of his ingenious machinations.

If Rowena thought of anything, it was the letter she would have to write to David telling him about the marriage. This was something she would have to do as soon as she could bring herself to do it, and she hoped for some inspiration to enable her to explain the extraordinary circumstances that would account for the unseemly hurried marriage without apprising him of the true state of affairs.

To the weary Rowena the reception seemed to

go on for ages, and she longed for the end of what had seemed to her to be the longest day of her life, and not even the thought of finding herself alone with the man she now heartily disliked could prevent her wishing the guests elsewhere.

As yet she had no idea where her 'lodgings', as Sean had termed it, would be, and when at last the guests started drifting off in the early evening, she was obliged to wait for his return after seeing some close friends of his off, actually going with them to their transport, and no doubt, Rowena thought bitterly, receiving some commiserations for his heroic leap into the unknown!

Having nothing else to do, she started idly clearing up the debris in the ballroom, and was startled by a stern voice stating, 'We'll see to that, Mrs Tancred,' and looked up to meet the disapproving eyes of Mrs Broom, who looked suitably shocked at seeing the master's wife carrying out such mundane tasks.

Rowena sighed inwardly, and left the rest of the plates that she had been neatly stacking ready to be collected and taken to the kitchen for washing-up, and for a moment or so she watched Mrs Broom and the two helpers who had now arrived to assist in the clearing up operation, but as she felt the surreptitious glances directed at her by the women as they worked, she quickly left the ballroom and made her way towards the hall, hoping that Sean was still around and had not decided to work off his distaste for the situation he had been forced to accept along with an unwanted bride.

As Rowena entered the hall, Sean came through the outer door and as he caught sight of her his strong mouth twisted slightly in an expression of irritation at her presence. 'That went off very well, Mrs Tancred,' he said tauntingly, with an emphasis on the name, and Rowena knew that he would always address her as 'Mrs Tancred' and never by her Christian name. It would be just another way of getting at her and reminding her that she had only bought the name and nothing else.

A delicate flush tinted her pale features as her eyes met his cold ones and she looked away quickly before she asked in an indifferent voice, 'Would you please tell me which room you've given me?' and this time it was her turn to add an emphasis on the word 'given' telling him that she fully understood her position and there had been no need for him to remind her.

As she watched a small muscle start to pulsate at the side of his mouth, Rowena felt a spurt of satisfaction at his fury in failing to annoy her. It was a game that he would soon grow tired of, since she did not intend to give him the satisfaction of knowing how easily she could be hurt; things were bad enough without entering into open warfare.

'I'll get Mrs Broom to show you to your quarters,' he said after an appreciable pause made to make her feel uncomfortable, and it had the desired effect, only Rowena was not going to let him know this.

Her wide brown eyes that didn't quite focus met the bright blue ones of Sean as she replied crisply, 'Is that necessary? Mrs Broom has enough to do at the moment without running after me. Just tell me where you've put me, and I'll make my own way there.'

Sean gave an indifferent shrug. 'On the left of the picture gallery you'll find a suite of rooms. Used to be the old nursery,' he added softly, 'and now obsolete, and not of enough historical value to warrant it being listed in the tour of the house.'

At the mention of the nursery Rowena felt her flush deepen and wished that she could sink through the floor and out of sight of this all-too-knowing character who could not have missed her embarrassment at this disclosure, and her fingers itched to slap his arrogant face. He could have put her in any one of a dozen rooms, and in a house of that size there must have been at least three suites in the new wing added during the last century to give the family more up-to-date facilities and provide them with some privacy, for the old house had long been noted for its antiquity, and although not officially opened to the public, had been visited by various groups of architectural students. All this Rowena had read about when she was still suffering from the pangs of adolescent love, eager to devour any item that concerned the home of her knight.

What privacy could she expect with people milling around the gallery on the open days? she asked herself bitterly. By placing her in the old nursery, Sean had scored a double hit at her sensitivity, although she doubted if this had occurred to him, for it was a faculty he would not credit her with. Being forced to live in the quarters that in bygone days had been haunted by the laughter of children and now fallen into disuse was bad enough, without being made to feel an unwanted encumbrance that had to slip in and out of her rooms avoiding the glances of the ever-curious visitors on tour of the house, feeling like a ghost returning to its haunt!

Rowena drew in a deep breath. 'Thank you,' she said in a small tight voice. 'At least it's a relief to know I'm in the house, and not in the stables!'

Sean's handsome brow darkened, and Rowena was certain that he had been about to take a step forward but pulled himself up in time. His strong lean hands clenched by his side and she knew he had very nearly struck her. 'I should watch your step if I were you,' he said softly, 'or you might get more than you bargained for, and it's got nothing to do with attraction, I can assure you. It will do you good to have to mind your manners. I'm not your father, but I'm willing to knock a modicum of respect for your betters into you when the occasion calls. To me you're the grocer's daughter and nothing else, so if you've any pipe dreams for the future you'd better forget them. I gave you ample warning of how it would be, and you'd do well to bear this in mind.'

Rowena hardly trusted herself to reply to these scathing words, and contented herself with a stiff formal, 'You'll have no worries on that score, I can promise you!' before turning away from him and walked towards the staircase before he could reply, holding her head high and strongly resisting the urge to take to her heels, she made her way to the gallery.

On inspection of the suite that was to be her new home, Rowena was surprised to find that the whole suite had been redecorated, and at some earlier time, obviously long before the event of her marriage, and she assumed that it must have been

done to accommodate some relation of Sean's, or
perhaps an old retainer of theirs, but none of this
had he told her, so she could be forgiven for
assuming the worst and expecting to find herself
wandering around in the middle of discarded
schoolroom artifacts. She gave a tight smile as she
recalled Sean's reaction to her remarks about the
stables. No wonder he had been so furious, for she
doubted if any other suite in the old house had
been as well cared for as the one she was standing
in.

As her eyes rested on a very old, but well kept
bureau in the corner of the lounge, and went on to
take in the rest of the furnishings, she wondered if
she ought to apologise to him for what was now
an unseemly and definitely uncalled for comment
on her future residence, but on recalling the remarks he had made before he had deigned to tell
her which suite she would be occupying, Rowena
lost all desire to attempt to make amends. Had he
not told her that the suite was once the old nursery, she would never have known its past use for
all traces of its history had now been eradicated,
but he had not been able to resist the chance of
making her feel uncomfortable.

Her small chin lifted as she recalled his scathing
comments on her being the grocer's daughter.
Such a comment might have found its mark with
her father, but Rowena had no such grandiose
pretensions, and grocer's daughter as she certainly
was, she had been brought up to mind her manners, in spite of what that detestable man thought
of her. In time to come he would surely know this,
she thought grimly, and she did not intend to let

him browbeat her in any way.

Rowena's eyes were bleak as she tried to imagine her future and what she was going to do with herself in her unwanted capacity as the squire's wife. Not that anyone would actually think of her as such, she was the golden ticket of prosperity for the last of the Tancreds, and the village benefactor for a forward-looking future that left them no worries of bulldozers tearing up their beautiful countryside.

With a sigh of exasperation Rowena walked over to the lounge window and stood gazing out. Directly below her was the stable area, and beyond that the park that surrounded the house, and beyond the park, the woods that she had roamed with Goldie.

At the thought of Goldie she gave a slight start; she had asked her father to see that she was sent up to Tancred House after the wedding, and goodness knew where she had been left, she thought, as she rushed into her bedroom and changed out of her finery, slipped on her corduroys and a light cashmere jumper, and went in search of her.

When she got down to the hall again there was no sign of Goldie, and surely this would be where she would find her, she thought worriedly. From the hall she went to the ballroom where Mrs Broom and her helpers were still hard at it, restoring the room to its former glory, and the hum of the vacuum cleaners would have successfully drowned any enquiry Rowena might have made about her pet, so she left them to it, hoping to eventually come across Goldie without disturbing anyone.

After a fruitless search through the whole of the ground floor, and finding no sign of Goldie, Rowena began to wonder if her father had forgotten her request to bring her to Tancred House and decided that that must be the answer.

On her way out of the drawing room she saw a telephone and without a second thought rang through to Eagles' Roost.

On hearing Mrs Gany's cheerful voice on the other end of the line Rowena felt a wave of misery wash over her. At least Mrs Gany liked her and it was nice to know that she had one friend apart from Miss Heysham. 'Is Goldie there, Mrs Gany?' she asked quickly, before her emotions got the better of her.

'Sitting right next to me,' returned Mrs Gany comfortably. 'She's wondering where you are, I expect,' she went on. 'Oh, Rowena, what a lovely wedding it was! I've never seen so many flowers in the church——'

'I asked my father to send her up to me,' Rowena cut in quickly; she was in no mood for sentimentality of that kind. 'Would you remind him?' she asked. 'He could get that garage chappie, George someone, to run her up if he's busy,' she added.

'Oh,' Mrs Gany replied, sounding perplexed, 'she was sent up, but there seems to have been some muddle somewhere, because George brought her back again. I thought perhaps you hadn't had time to make arrangements for a place to keep her. At least, that's what Mr Tancred told George, and George said that he didn't look too pleased about it, either.'

There was a long pause on the line after this

while Rowena digested this latest autocratic action on Sean Tancred's part and what exactly she could do about it.

'Look, if it's awkward,' Mrs Gany said quickly, 'why not let her stay here? You can pick her up for her walks, just as you used to do.'

Rowena took a deep breath. 'For today, perhaps,' she replied firmly, 'while I make some arrangements, but I hope to be able to fetch her tomorrow. You'll give her her supper before you go, won't you?' she asked anxiously.

Mrs Gany assured her on this point, and after making a few more desultory remarks, Rowena was able to ring off.

Her hand shook slightly as she replaced the receiver, and fury built up inside her. How dared he send her dog away without even mentioning the matter to her? she thought furiously.

'I thought I'd made it quite clear that this part of the house should remain my private quarters,' Sean said in a hard voice behind her, and Rowena whirled round to face him.

'My apologies,' she replied, in an equally cutting voice. 'I came in search of my dog. As I couldn't find her I took the liberty of using the phone to ring home and find out what had happened to her.'

'There's a telephone in your lounge, in case you hadn't noticed,' he returned with a sneer in his voice, 'but I guess any excuse is better than none.'

Rowena's hands clenched by her side and she fervently wished she was nearer the small table in front of her and able to reach the ornaments on it so that she could throw one at him. 'I hear you sent Goldie back,' she got out in a low level voice, in spite of her churning emotions as her shocked senses registered the meaning behind his last words. 'I want my dog with me,' she asserted grimly. 'I have no intention of leaving her with my father.'

For a second in time her brown eyes, now flashing sparks of fury, clashed with the icy blue ones of Sean. 'And where do you intend to keep the animal?' he asked haughtily.

'With me, in my quarters,' Rowena replied steadily, her eyes holding his contemptuous gaze to show him that she did not intend to give an inch on this matter.

'I do not approve of animals in the house,' he said autocratically. 'You can keep it in the stables if you insist—otherwise, there's nothing doing,' he added adamantly.

Rowena thought of the ramshackle stables and the roofs that probably leaked when it rained, and almost shivered at the thought of Goldie lying on a sack in that deserted area. 'What heating is there out there?' she demanded, knowing the answer.

Sean's haughty blond eyebrows rose. 'None,' he replied bitingly. 'If the dog's healthy, it should come to no harm.'

'She's only eight months old,' Rowena answered firmly, 'and sleeps in the kitchen at home. April can be a very cold month,' she added significantly.

His only reply to this was an offhand shrug, and Rowena knew he was not going to be moved on this point, but she had to try anyway.

'Look,' she said swiftly, 'I promise she won't get in anyone's way. There's ample room in my suite

for her. She's used to company and won't understand if she's shut away——' Her voice broke
slightly on the last sentence. She was unhappy
enough without having the worry of Goldie
pushed out in the cold.

'That's another thing you should have thought
about,' he answered harshly. 'Labradors are gun-
dogs, not lapdogs. She'll do well enough in the stables after she gets over the initial shock of not
being made a fuss of. That's my last word. Now
if there's nothing else you want, I'm expecting
company.'

Rowena turned abruptly and went to the door
without giving him another look. She was too
choked to say anything, and made her way back to
her rooms and shut the door firmly behind her.

By now the tears were gushing down her cheeks.
Until then she had not realised how much she had
been depending on Goldie's company and who
would be her only ally in that huge old house that
neither welcomed her nor wanted her.

For the next hour Rowena busied herself with
odd jobs. She unpacked her suitcases that had
been left in her bedroom, a task that she had put
off until the last minute, because it meant a kind
of finality and an end to all her hopes for release
from her impossible situation.

When she had finished the unpacking she stood
in the middle of the bedroom and gazed around
her. The thick gold ring on her third finger felt as
alien as the room. It was like living in an hotel, she
thought bitterly. All conveniences, and very impersonal. There was even a small dining room to
complete her isolation from the rest of the house—

not that Rowena would complain about that—to have to take meals with a man like Sean Tancred didn't bear thinking about, and she was only too grateful to be spared such a happening.

She then wandered into the lounge and in a completely abstracted manner rearranged the furniture, not caring for the too-formal previous arrangement that made the room look like a set piece for a magazine advertisement for fine living, and dragged what looked like, and very probably was, a Hepplewhite sofa from its previous position against the window wall and into a more homely-looking position opposite the ornate fireplace that now held an electric imitation log fire and although the type of fire selected suited its surroundings, it still looked out of place to Rowena.

Two wingbacked, grand-looking chairs then came under her attention, and not liking their position either, she moved them closer into the room and placed them opposite each other on either side of the fireplace, and finally placing one of the small occasional tables against the end of the sofa, stood back to survey her efforts and was pleased with the result. The room now had a cosy and intimate atmosphere, and when she had added a few of her personal possessions, such as ornaments, and that picture of David's that she intended to collect the following day, she could almost imagine herself being happy there—as happy, she thought bleakly, as it was possible to be in such circumstances.

Her physical efforts had exhausted her, but she had needed to do something to take her mind off that last encounter with Sean Tancred and his adamant refusal to let her keep Goldie with her in her rooms.

In spite of the fact that it was April and theoretically spring, Rowena switched on the electric fire, as the room was chilly, and this action inevitably brought back the question of Goldie and how she would fare in the stables. With any luck she might howl all night and keep a certain detestable man awake, and exasperated enough to go back on his word!

A tap on the door broke through Rowena's wishful thinking and she took a deep breath before calling out, 'Come in,' afraid that her visitor would be the last person she wanted to see, but to her relief it was Mrs Broom who entered, carrying a tray that she put down on the small side table by the sofa where Rowena was seated. 'I expect you could do with some supper,' she commented quietly, before she turned to leave the room.

Rowena gave her a surprised look and noticed how tired she looked. There had been a lot of cleaning up to do. 'I could have come down for something, Mrs Broom,' she said. 'I don't expect to be waited on.' Her frank eyes met the housekeeper's tired blue ones. 'There's a service hatch in the dining-room, isn't there?' she added. 'Just tell me what times the meals are, and I'll collect them from the hatch. There's certainly no need for you to cart everything up—failing that, that is if the hatch isn't working—I'll come and collect it.'

The look of relief on Mrs Broom's face was not missed by Rowena, but she still hesitated. 'Well, if you've no objection to such an arrangement,' she demurred slowly.

'No objection whatsoever,' Rowena cut in firmly. 'In fact I insist upon it.'

Mrs Broom's reply was an abrupt nod of her greying brown head signifying approval of this arrangement, and she gave Rowena what she could only interpret as a sympathetic look before she turned to leave.

'Oh, before you go, Mrs Broom, I'm having my puppy brought here.' She looked away from the housekeeper's curious eyes before she added, 'She'll sleep in the stables. The only thing is, I shall have to worry you for some warm milk in the evenings, if that's no bother,' she ended lamely.

'No bother at all,' Mrs Broom replied swiftly. 'Used to dogs, I am. There was always an animal around, until Mr Sean lost his spaniel, that is.'

Rowena wished she had the courage to ask her where the dog had slept and suspected that it was in the house and not in the isolated stables, but forced herself to stay silent. It was bad enough that Mrs Broom obviously felt sorry for her, without giving her more cause for sympathy.

When the door closed behind Mrs Broom, Rowena sat for a long moment staring into the bright revolving lights of the log fire. Would the housekeeper now return to the kitchen and to her supper that she would probably share with her two helpers, and then settle down for a cosy chat? If so, Rowena could well imagine the subject under discussion—the new bride and how uncomfortable she must be feeling—not to mention disappointed at the outcome of the marriage!

She gave a deep sigh. If only they knew, she thought wearily, that she would be a sight more uncomfortable—she gave a wry grimace—uncomfortable was not the right word; terrified was nearer the mark, should it have been a real marriage.

After managing to eat a few of the thin sandwiches that Mrs Broom had so thoughtfully provided, and one cup of tea, since she was neither hungry nor thirsty, but felt she had to make the effort for the housekeeper's sake if nothing else, Rowena took the tray through to the dining room and placed it in the service hatch and sent it down to the kitchen, noticing with no small relief that the hatch was in perfect working order.

Going back into the lounge again, she curled herself up on the sofa and glancing up at the ornate clock on the mantelpiece in front of her saw that it was eight-thirty, and wondered how she was going to spend the rest of the evening. As her glance fell on the large television placed in the corner of the room she gave another grimace; she was not an addict of that particular form of amusement.

In the days to come, she presumed, she would find ways of amusing herself. She was well used to loneliness as far as companionship went, but this had been cushioned to a certain degree by her secretarial duties that had kept her occupied most mornings and on the odd occasion during the afternoon too, if her father was in the process of securing yet another shop, for although he was supposed to be retired, he still kept an iron hold on the business, and only delegated normal routine work to his managers.

After a short while she felt a drowsiness creeping over her. It had been an exhausting day for her, mentally as well as physically. Tomorrow was another day, and perhaps she would be able to persuade her father to let her carry on as his secretary, since nothing had been said about this, and he needed secretarial help and there was certainly no reason why she should not carry on as before. It would give her somewhere to go, a haven from the unfamiliar surroundings she was now in. She could, she thought sleepily, take Goldie out in the afternoons just as she used to. Mrs Gany would be sure to rustle her up some lunch.

The sharp ringing of the telephone brought her out of her drowsy musings, and sitting up she stared at it as if surprised to find it in the same room, and as it kept on ringing she was forced to answer it, although she did not think the call was for her.

Her timid, 'Hello?' was answered by Sean's irritable, 'Your father's on the line. When you've finished, will you give him the number on your telephone for any future calls,' the next minute her father's voice came over the line.

'Rowena? I forgot to tell you that I'm going up to town tomorrow for a week. I've given Mrs Gany the week off, but I gather she's got stuck with that dog of yours, so you'd better work something out by tomorrow. See Sean about it, no doubt he'll fix something up. That fool of a handyman brought it back with him, so I heard from Mrs Gany.'

It was hardly the handyman's fault, Rowena thought wearily, that the owner of the house refused to accept Goldie, but she said nothing of this. 'I'll collect her tomorrow,' she replied, and added quickly before he rang off, 'Leave what you've got in the typing line in the tray, and anything else you want done.'

'You can forget about all that from now on,' her father replied firmly. 'You'll have enough to do without worrying about that sort of thing. Things are different now,' he added with a hint of pride in his voice.

On hearing the click on the other end of the line, Rowena almost slammed her receiver down in her frustration. How were things different? she thought furiously. Apart from the fact that she was called 'Mrs Tancred' and living in Tancred House, things were exactly the same, and she couldn't see why she couldn't carry on as before. It wasn't as if anything else was expected of her except to keep out of Sean Tancred's way, and what better way was there of doing that than giving Tancred House a wide berth during the day?

She frowned as she recalled what her father had said about going to town. Mrs Gany had said nothing of this when she had spoken to her barely an hour ago, and she gave a deep sigh. It was just like her father to suddenly decide to drop in at the office like that. It was a disconcerting habit of his, but it did ensure that the staff were kept on their toes, and that was precisely his reasoning too!

So that settled it, she thought dully. Even if she had been tempted to keep Goldie at Eagles' Roost, things had now been taken out of her hands. Goldie would have to stay in the stables. First thing tomorrow she would have to find a warm spot for her to sleep—if there was such a place, she thought scathingly, and felt another surge of dislike towards Sean Tancred. It was certainly a case of 'love me, love my dog', and the disdain he held for her automatically included her pet.

CHAPTER FIVE

AFTER breakfast the following morning, Rowena went to the stables fervently hoping that she would not encounter Sean and that whatever work he had been doing out there that day she had made the mistake of going to see him was now completed, and that he had other things to attend to, preferably away from the vicinity of Tancred House.

Her luck held as she entered the stabling area, where all was quiet and there was no sign of activity, and she gave a slight shiver as she passed out of the pale sunlit yard into the dark confines of the stables.

As she glanced up at the roof above her she gave a grimace. She had been right about the leaking roof, for she could see a small shaft of daylight high above her, and surmised that many years had passed since any attention had been paid to these old outbuildings, and did not hold out much hope of finding a dry and draught-proofed spot in which to leave Goldie.

In the end she settled for the last stall on the

right, simply because it was the only one that still had a workable lower hatch that would confine Goldie and lessen her fears of her wandering around the area, yelping her indignation at finding herself in such inhospitable surroundings, particularly after the comfort of a warm kitchen. She would yelp anyway, Rowena thought miserably, and her eyes were bleak as she surveyed the stone flooring at her feet and through which she could feel the cold rising.

With a shrug of resignation she set about cleaning out the stall. With an ancient broom and equally old bucket that she had found in what she supposed was once the tack room, and filling the bucket from an outside pump, she set to work, glad of something to do to relieve her pent-up feelings.

'What the devil——?' queried a cold voice that made her swish the water out of the stall with more exuberance than was called for and narrowly miss Sean's immaculate brown cords, 'I swept that area clean only a few days ago,' he commented pithily. 'I presume it's where you intend to keep the animal, is it?' he demanded, when Rowena chose to ignore his remarks, hoping that he would go away, 'only I had my eye on this stall for a mare I'm purchasing,' he went on in a soft goading voice.

When this last remark eventually reached through to Rowena, who had told herself not to take any notice of what he might say about her labours and to simply ignore him, her good resolutions were abandoned and she glared at him. 'You might have mentioned that when you said that I could keep Goldie here,' she replied furiously.

'So I'm telling you now,' he said smoothly. 'What's wrong with the first stall?' he queried haughtily.

'Everything!' Rowena got out between clenched teeth. 'In case you haven't noticed, the roof leaks just above it. Also, the hatch is practically off its hinges and I'm not keeping Goldie on a chain to keep her in. This is the only stall with a hatch that works, and it's dry,' and she added bitterly, 'I might have known I'd choose the wrong one!' and threw the broom down on the floor to emphasise her feelings.

'I was taught to leave things as I found them,' he said caustically, looking pointedly at the broom.

'Well, in that case——' Rowena snapped, as she picked up the broom and marched out of the stall to where a heap of damp and definitely muddy straw lay ready to be disposed of, and swept it all back into the stall, making sure that it was evenly scattered over the stone floor. She knew she was being childish, but her fury drove her on.

Sean gave her a long look before he transferred his attention to what had once been a sparkling clean area, and was now streaked with mud and wet straw, and raised his brows. 'Well, if that's the state you want to keep your animal in, I suppose it's up to you,' he commented haughtily, and strode out of the stable.

Rowena's hands clenched round the broom handle and had it been of a more brittle wood she would have snapped it. What had he meant by that? Was he saying that she could have the stall for Goldie? Her eyes swept round the small enclosure, taking in the muddy area that she would now have to clean again if she wanted to bring Goldie back that morning, and tears of utter frustration filled her eyes. He must have enjoyed her show of temper, particularly when he knew that she would have to clean it up again. She wouldn't put it past him to still claim the stall for his mare, she thought acidly, as she began the cleaning up operation. He might just have said that to make her repair the damage. Either way, she couldn't win, she thought wearily, and got on with her task.

By the time she had collected Goldie, her father had left for London, although it was only a little after nine-thirty.

'She is pleased to see you, isn't she?' Mrs Gany commented, as Rowena received Goldie's exuberant greetings at the sight of her mistress, yelping her delight at her appearance. 'I took her out for a short walk yesterday,' Mrs Gany went on, as she dried the breakfast dishes. 'I suppose you know your father took it into his head to spend a few days in London,' she remarked, as she stacked the clean crockery away in the cupboard.

'He rang me last night,' replied Rowena, as she collected Goldie's feeding bowl and blanket, and taking a carrier bag out of the kitchen dresser drawer started filling it with her pet's belongings, having to wrestle with her for her favourite toy, her rubber bone.

'Like packing for a baby, isn't it?' commented Mrs Gany with a smile as she watched Rowena carefully checking to see if she had got everything.

'That I wouldn't know,' replied Rowena with an attempt at levity, and it was not until she had said that that she realised the significance of her words, and quickly turned away and rechecked the contents of the bag. 'Don't let me keep you, Mrs Gany, if you want to get away. You've got a key, haven't you? I just want to collect a few things to take back with me. I'll lock up afterwards. Father is a nuisance,' she added thoughtfully. 'I mean, he didn't give you much notice, did he? It doesn't give you much time to plan anything, does it?' she asked.

Mrs Gany smiled. 'Well, as a matter of fact it suited me fine,' she said confidentially. 'I've got my sister staying with me at the moment, and this break means I'll be able to take a few trips out with her. She'll be delighted,' she added happily. 'She's a widow too, and housekeeps for a family in Berkshire. Her people are away on one of those luxury cruises at the moment, and she always comes to me on her holidays.'

'Oh, good,' said Rowena, and she meant it, for she remembered Mrs Gany once telling her that although she had an adequate pension, she needed to go out to work just to fill the time in. Her small cottage was only a short walk down the hill from Eagles' Roost, which suited her and her employer, otherwise it would have had to have been a living-in post, but as things were, she finished around nine o'clock in the evenings, but was willing to stay longer when the occasion called, such as a dinner party.

When Rowena was assured that she had everything that Goldie would need, she went in search of her personal effects, and on her way back through the drawing-room she collected David's picture, certain that her father would not miss it, and if he did, he would not comment on the fact, for he had never changed his thoughts in that direction. To him, artists were no better than long-haired layabouts, shirking a more responsible position in life.

By the time Rowena left Eagles' Roost she was fairly loaded. In one hand she clutched the bag containing Goldie's effects, and in the other a large straw shopping bag in which she had placed David's picture and the few cherished possessions that she had, such as a framed photograph of her mother that had stood on her dressing-table, and with Goldie straining on the leash raring to start off on their new adventure, she was relieved when they reached the end of their journey.

It was not until she reached Tancred House that she found that she had another problem on her hands. She could not go straight to her rooms, not with Goldie, and that meant that she would have to carry everything round to the stables first, install Goldie in her new quarters and then dash back to the house and leave her things in her rooms, then go back to collect Goldie and take her for her walk.

It was all so stupid, and this was only the beginning, she thought crossly, as she passed the imposing front of Tancred House and paused to ease the weight of the straw bag in her right hand and transfer it to her left, giving the huge studded door a glance of dislike as she did so, and it was then that she conceived the notion of leaving her things in the hall of the house and pick them up later, after she had taken Goldie out.

With Goldie securely tied to an iron stanchion by the side of the door, Rowena slipped quickly into the house and placed the straw bag in the first available space she saw, then rushed back to collect Goldie, who had just started to vent her indignation at being left on her own just when she thought she was out for a walk.

Rowena then proceeded to the stables and introduced Goldie to her new quarters, which she inspected with much enthusiasm and in happy ignorance of the purpose behind the visit. While Goldie rushed around exploring every nook and cranny within sniffing distance, Rowena unpacked the carrier containing her blanket and water bowl and placed them in the stall, then put the puppy meal and grooming tools on a shelf above the stall, reminding herself that she would have to pay the butcher a visit as soon as possible; she had enough for that day but not enough for the next. She would also, she thought with a grimace, have to beg a place in which to keep her pet's food from Mrs Broom, although she did not anticipate any trouble there. On the face of things, she had the housekeeper's sympathy which would smooth the way for any small requests providing they were reasonable.

Goldie's walk was next on the agenda, and Rowena stayed out a good deal longer than she usually did, arriving back at the stables just before twelve, when Mrs Broom had said lunch would be served.

A crescendo of indignant yelps followed her all the way back to the house, and she winced as the yelps turned to a hurt whining tone from the bewildered Goldie. She would just have to get used to it, Rowena thought—in fact they would both have to get used to it. After lunch she would beg

some milk from Mrs Broom and give her her
midday snack, and afterwards? She shrugged; another walk, perhaps, to take Goldie's mind off her
troubles, and she was glad it was a fine day although the wind was a bit on the chilly side.

Rowena might have known that she had had her
share of luck where Sean was concerned, for as
soon as she walked into the house she ran into
him, but her concentration was fixed on the apparent disappearance of her shopping bag, which was
nowhere to be seen. 'Have you seen a straw bag?'
she demanded. 'I left it here in the hall this morning.'

'Oh, so it was yours, was it?' he replied tersely. 'I
nearly fell over it. I might have known. You've got
a habit of leaving things around, I notice. Mrs
Broom's got enough to do without running about
after you,' he added waspishly.

Rowena's eyes opened wide in indignation. 'I do
not leave things lying around,' she replied crossly,
'and I wouldn't have left the bag in the hall, only I
had Goldie with me and saw no sense in dragging
it to the stables with me. Where is it, then?' she
asked brusquely, staring round the large expanse
of the hall to locate it.

'In the recess where it's out of the way,' he replied, and pointed a long lean forefinger towards a
hidden recess behind the door.

'Thank you,' Rowena said icily, and going to
collect it, gave a gasp of annoyance when she saw
that the bag had not been placed on the ledge in
the recess but, judging by its crooked position, had
been flung there.

Her first worry was whether the glass on her

mother's photograph was still intact, and when she was assured of this, she turned her attention to David's picture, taking it out and critically examining it, then she gave a sigh of relief on finding that too was still intact. It might not have been, though, she thought furiously. Hadn't Sean also been taught to look after other people's possessions? A fine one he was, to criticise her!

'That's not bad at all,' commented Sean, who had followed her into the recess and now stood looking over her shoulder at David's painting, and Rowena, who had been startled by his close proximity when she thought he had left the hall, watched his gaze travel over the scene portrayed and rest finally on the signature below, only the surname being legible. 'Yours?' he asked with a hint of disbelief in his voice.

'Of course not!' Rowena replied briskly, again showing her indignation.

'Not your father's?' he asked, and this time the disbelief was more pronounced. 'I don't somehow see him as the arty type.'

Rowena shook her head impatiently, and a strand of her dark hair lightly brushed Sean's cheek. She did not know this, so she did not know the reason why he stepped back from her, but was only too pleased that he had done so. The man disturbed her, and it was nothing to do with romantic fancies either. 'David,' she said. 'My brother. I do have a brother, you know,' she tacked on sarcastically.

Sean nodded. 'So you have,' he commented dryly. 'I seem to recall him. A tall blond boy, isn't he? Used to stand with you and watch us play cricket, didn't he?' he queried with a hint of a sneer in his voice.

Rowena could not meet his insolent look, for she knew only too well what he was referring to, and how she used to hang around just for a glimpse of her hero when she was younger. She wondered vaguely if he realised just how cruel he was being. She might still have a crush on him, in fact he thought she had—so he was being cruel— trying to get at her where it hurt most, and how vulnerable she was, not in the romantic interest, but in her pride. 'That's right,' she replied quietly, and her large eyes that didn't quite focus looked even more distant as they met his blue ones. Then she turned away from him and put the picture back in the bag, then picked it up and turned to leave.

'I don't remember seeing him at the wedding,' Sean went on, determined it seemed to go on plaguing her. 'He was invited, surely?'

Rowena gave him a weary look. 'As a matter of fact, he wasn't,' she said, still in that quiet reserved voice. 'He's spending the vacation on a hiking tour of the Highlands and we couldn't contact him. I shall have to write to him and tell him,' she added firmly, and this time she was allowed to leave and made her way back to her rooms.

On Monday, after spending most of Sunday in the stables with Goldie trying to get her to settle down in what to her must have seemed like solitary confinement, Rowena seriously considered going to see Miss Heysham and begging a week's boarding for her pet until her father returned home and Mrs Gany could look after her.

It was all very well for Sean to say that she had been spoilt and as a gundog she ought not to be coddled, but the fact remained that Goldie was still a puppy, and if she had been spoilt, and Rowena would not concede this, then it was hardly the dog's fault.

The minute Rowena turned the corner from the house to the stables, she could hear Goldie's yelps and miserably surmised that she hadn't stopped since she had left her the previous evening.

If anything, it was colder than it had been the previous day, and Rowena shivered in her light parka, wishing she had chosen a thicker sweater to wear under it, and fervently hoped that Goldie's misery was not added to by the cold damp atmosphere, although she ought to have been warm enough snuggled up in the thick straw that Rowena had put down for her.

'It's all right, pet,' she crooned as Goldie threw herself at her. 'I'm going to do something about it. I only hope Miss Heysham can oblige, that's all,' she said softly, as she fondled her pet's golden head, and noted with no little alarm that her eyes were running. After feeling her nose and finding it warm and when Goldie refused the warm milk that Rowena had kept in a flask overnight for her her alarm increased. 'It's the vet for you this morning,' she said firmly, as she tried to coax Goldie into taking some of the milk.

'It's probably only a chill,' Mr Sawyer said, shortly after nine that morning, for an anxious Rowena had been first in the queue, arriving fifteen minutes before the start of surgery. 'Just keep her warm. I'll give her a shot of penicillin to be on

the safe side,' he went on, 'and if she doesn't perk
up bring her back on Thursday.' He gave the still
worried-looking Rowena a smile. 'Puppies are like
babies,' he said soothingly, 'up one moment, down
the next. They've a great recovery rate. She'll
probably be galloping around in an hour's time,'
he added comfortably.

Not if she had to stay in that cold stable, thought
Rowena unhappily, and certainly not if she had to
be kept warm.

As she left the veterinary surgery, her thoughts
were on Miss Heysham. She had no choice now
but to take Goldie along there and hope that she
would agree to keep her until her father returned.

Fate it seemed was not being kind to Rowena
that morning, for when she arrived at Miss Heysham's cottage she was informed by her next-door
neighbour, who happened to be cleaning her windows as Rowena arrived, that Miss Heysham was
away that week. 'Gone to those friends of hers in
York,' she said cheerfully. 'Lovely wedding,' she
went on conversationally, 'and no stinting on the
liquid refreshments either, as my John said,' she
added with a grin of appreciation.

Rowena's thoughts were not exactly compli-
mentary on this subject, and she murmured
something on the lines that she was glad that they
had enjoyed it, and made her escape before she
became bogged down in further conversation.

What on earth was she to do now? she wondered frantically, and considered sneaking Goldie
up to her rooms and keeping her hidden away
until she was better, but as soon as the idea was
formed she abandoned it. She would have to go

out some time, and the chance of completely avoiding Sean Tancred on such furtive expeditions was practically non-existent. He had an annoying knack of appearing just when she least wanted to see him.

Her smooth brow was creased in thought as she walked on her way with Goldie, who now seemed to have perked up a bit and was straining at the leash hoping to be let off at the earliest opportunity. What if she tackled Sean about it, and told him that Goldie had a chill and what the vet had said about keeping her warm—would he let her keep her in the house?

As the vision of his cold eyes and haughty expression rose before her, Rowena almost shook her head. He would point out with his usual arrogance that as a normally healthy dog, she would get over it, in other words, she was making a fuss over nothing!

Why had her father to choose that week to go away? she thought miserably. If she could have kept Goldie there all her problems would have been solved. She stopped in her tracks as a thought suddenly struck her. What was the matter with her? Of course she could still keep Goldie there! She had her key, hadn't she? All she had to do was to call in on Mrs Gany and explain the situation to her, so that she knew what was going on and wouldn't think there was an intruder in the house if she happened to spot signs of life there.

Rowena's step was considerably lighter as she made her way to Mrs Gany's house, hoping that she had not left on some expedition with her sister, and her mouth relaxed into a smile as she heard someone approaching from the other side of the door after she had rung the bell.

From the appearance of the housekeeper with her coat on, Rowena knew she had been only just in time to catch her before she went out, and she made her explanation as short as possible so as not to hold her up in case she had a bus to catch, ending with, 'So you see, as everything is so muddled at the moment, and Goldie has this chill, I thought it would be better if I kept her at Eagles' Roost.'

To Rowena's relief, Mrs Gany accepted what must have seemed a very odd request considering that Rowena now lived at Tancred House, an establishment several times the size of Eagles' Roost, but as Mrs Gany heartily assured her that she thought that was a very good idea, and did she want her to order some milk for Goldie—she was going past the dairy that morning—the fact did not escape Rowena that the kindly housekeeper had an inkling as to how things were her end. She had known about Goldie being sent back by the autocratic Sean and had obviously drawn her own conclusions on the matter. 'I could pop up and see her settled in the evenings,' she told Rowena. 'It will be no bother, we're only out during the day,' she added kindly.

'Please don't do any such thing,' Rowena replied quickly. 'I have no intention of spoiling your holiday, and Father would be furious. I've got it all worked out, I shall keep her with me until she's got over this chill—and the chances are that I shall have to leave her with you next week, on the basis of what you suggested earlier, and come back to exercise her as I used to do—until, that is, I can get something worked out my end,' she went on firmly as she saw the sympathy in the house-keeper's eyes on that last flat statement.

'Well, if you're sure,' hesitated Mrs Gany, and at Rowena's firm nod she added, 'You've only to say, you know, and I'll see she's all right for you.'

'I'm sure,' Rowena confirmed. 'You go ahead and enjoy your holiday, and I promise to let you know if things get awkward my end, although I don't anticipate any trouble. Oh, will you make it a pint a day,' she added as an afterthought before she left her, for the thought had just occurred to her that there was no reason why she shouldn't stay at her old home as well. It wasn't as if her presence was needed at Tancred House, she was a free agent when all was said and done, but she said nothing of this to Mrs Gany, and repeating her hope that she had a good week, she left her.

As Rowena walked up the hill towards Eagles' Roost, her mind was busy with her plans, and she was looking forward to her week back at her old home as one looks forward to some longed-for holiday. The only one likely to oppose her plan was her father, who had kept his head firmly en-trenched in the sand where her marriage was con-cerned, refusing to acknowledge the possibility of his making a mistake, and certain that all would be well in time. She gave a wry grimace at these thoughts, recalling his words that she was a woman, wasn't she, and would find ways of cap-tivating her husband.

He hadn't, she thought sadly, even bothered to ascertain whether she wanted any such alliance with the man she had married, and no amount of

protestations on this point would have got
through to him even if he had sought such confirmation. She sighed, as she let herself into her old
home. Well, he didn't have to know that she had
been there that week. Mrs Gany was not likely to
mention it to him as her father was not one for
chats, and even if the opportunity did arise,
Rowena was sure Mrs Gany would keep her own
counsel on the matter.

Goldie seemed as delighted as her mistress was
at being back home again, and soon settled in her
usual place in the kitchen although her blanket
was missing. 'We'll have to go back and get it,' she
told Goldie, whose large head now rested on her
paws, and her brown eyes followed Rowena's
movements as she foraged in the larder to check
on supplies and make a note of what she would
need for the week, and get them on the way back
from Tancred House after collecting Goldie's
effects.

As soon as Rowena had made out a list of what
she wanted, she put Goldie on the lead again and
set off for Tancred House.

Her pet's enthusiasm for the walk noticeably
waned as they turned into the long drive to the
house. 'I know exactly how you feel,' Rowena
murmured to her, 'but at least your worries are
over. No more cold lodgings for you, pet!'

After collecting Goldie's things from the stable,
Rowena made her way back to the house and the
kitchen domain where she told Mrs Broom that she
would be away that week, and at her rather surprised blink at such news hastily explained the
reason, and was glad to be able to add the truth

that her father was away that week, and that she
would be keeping an eye on the house during his
absence.

It all sounded plausible enough, but Rowena
had an uncomfortable feeling that Mrs Broom,
like Mrs Gany, had put her own interpretation on
the matter, but Rowena was past caring, and
saying that she would be back on Sunday for
lunch, she made her escape.

As they headed away from Tancred House
Rowena felt a sense of relief and judging by the
way Goldie pulled on her leash as they left the pre-
cincts of the old house, her feelings were re-
ciprocated.

By the time they got back to Eagles' Roost,
Rowena was even more loaded with packages than
she had been on the journey to Tancred House not
more than twenty-four hours ago, but this time
with supplies for herself as well as Goldie.

Only when the door was firmly latched behind
her did Rowena let out a great sigh of relief. She
had a whole week ahead of her, away from the
hateful Sean and the sympathetic glances of Mrs
Broom, not that these worried her in the least, but
it would be nice to get back to some kind of nor-
mality, even for a short time.

She would write to David that evening, she
thought as she prepared Goldie's midday snack. It
would be easier to write the letter there than at
Tancred House, a place where she would never feel
at home, and heaven only knew how she was going
to cope in the future.

CHAPTER SIX

THE first two days of Rowena's week at her old home passed off peaceably. She had written to David and given him the bare news of the wedding but had not enlarged upon the subject, beginning with, 'I know this will surprise you.' He couldn't be more surprised than she herself had been to find herself entering upon such an alliance, she thought ironically, as she sought for the right words to explain the happening. Finally she gave it best, and entered into a sketchy description of her new home, hoping it sounded a lot more enthusiastic than her actual feelings for the historic old house, but at least it was something she could enlarge upon without having to watch her words. She ended the letter by asking him how he had enjoyed his holiday, sent her love, and with a sigh of relief sealed the letter in an envelope and addressed it to his London lodgings.

On the third day her peace was somewhat shattered by the arrival of Sean, who did not stop to ring the door bell but strode in on her unceremoniously and in a fine temper. 'So this is where you've hidden yourself, is it?' he snapped furiously. 'You might at least have done me the courtesy of letting me know your plans!'

Rowena was just as angry as he was. What right had he to come barging in on her like this? This

was her home—well, her father's home anyway,
she conceded angrily. 'I told Mrs Broom where I
was,' she said. 'If you'd asked her she would have
told you. And I'm not hiding myself away,' she
added crossly. 'I've a good reason for being here.
Goldie's got a chill and the vet said I was to keep
her warm. I wouldn't say the stables were warm,
would you?' she challenged him.

'I am not in the habit of expecting my housekeeper to keep me informed on matters of that
nature,' he replied angrily. 'As for the stables,
they're warm enough for a healthy animal,' he
added caustically. 'I doubt that it was a chill. She
probably worked herself up to a temperature fret-
ting. Only goes to prove what I said earlier about
her being spoilt,' he concluded autocratically, and
bent down to fondle Goldie's ears as she sidled up
to him and felt her nose. 'She looks perfectly
healthy to me,' he added, and gave the annoyed
Rowena a narrowed look. 'Not using her as an
excuse, are you?' he asked tauntingly.

Rowena's eyes opened a fraction wider as they
met his mocking ones. 'An excuse for what?' she
asked quietly.

'Oh, I think you know what I mean,' Sean
answered suavely. 'Things didn't exactly turn out
as you'd hoped, did they? Perhaps you thought
that if you did the disappearing act I might be
worried enough about you to decide to change the
status quo. Or perhaps something on the lines of
absence making the heart grow fonder?' he suggested silkily.

'What utter rot!' Rowena gasped, more in indignation than fury. 'Just what sort of an idiot do you

think I am?' she demanded, almost spluttering in her emotion. 'No, don't tell me, I can guess! I'm supposed to be so besotted by your manly charms that I've lost all sense of pride, and my sole aim in life is for you to make me your wife!' She stopped suddenly, horrified at what she had said, and her cheeks deepened in colour. This wasn't like her at all, she thought bewilderedly, as her shocked eyes met Sean's knowing ones and took in his wide grin that showed his white even teeth.

She took a deep breath. 'If you believe that, then you'll believe anything,' she went on quietly, and with a dignity that was more like her old self. 'You certainly won't believe me when I tell you that such a happening would be utterly abhorrent to me,' she gave a slight shudder, 'not only abhorrent,' she continued, making herself go on, 'but thoroughly distasteful. You see, I don't even like you. I stopped my childish daydreams about you years ago. One unkind remark cured all that nonsense, and I'm not likely to expose myself again, particularly on what I consider an unworthy cause,' she added vehemently, and met his eyes unflinchingly, her own full of scorn. 'If anyone's daydreaming, it's you,' she tacked on flatly.

Rowena felt a flash of triumph at the way Sean's eyes had narrowed to a slit on that last remark. He hadn't liked that one bit, she thought happily, inwardly revelling at getting some of her own back.

His reply completely knocked the complacent expression from her face. 'Suppose I wanted an heir?' he queried silkily.

Rowena shook her head as if unable to believe

the evidence of her ears, and stared back at him while she absorbed the shock he had just given her, her wide eyes registering the panic and confusion of her thoughts, and as she saw him smile again in that knowing way, she knew he was baiting her. By now she ought to have swooned at his feet at the very thought of being allowed such an honour. Not that he meant one word of it. He was just testing, still unable to believe that she disliked him.

'You would have to go to another supermarket,' she replied as steadily as she was able, but her small hands curled into fists that she would dearly have loved to pummel him with. 'This one doesn't cater for that sort of thing. Besides,' she added sarcastically, 'wouldn't that be rather a comedown for the auspicious name of Tancred? Just think of it—lots of little grocery boys rushing around those hallowed walls. There's not much that we have in common, but I think that we shall agree on that point.'

Sean stood regarding her with hooded eyes. 'Touché!' he said softly, making her glance quickly away from the blue fire of his eyes. 'Perhaps one day you'll discover that I'm not quite the snob that you think I am,' he added slowly, and just as quickly as he had introduced the subject, dropped it and brought up another. 'Now that the dog has recovered I presume you'll be coming back.' He strode towards the door as if that was that. He had come to collect a missing piece of luggage and having found it was making sure it was returned.

That was how Rowena saw it, and her fury rose at the thought that he regarded her as his property to command at will. 'I shall be returning on Sunday,' she replied firmly, and seeing the flash of annoyance this pronouncement produced in Sean, she went on quickly, 'Father's away for the week,' using his absence as an extra excuse.

'I happen to know that,' Sean grated, showing his impatience with her. 'I supplied him with the addresses of a few of my clubs. I shall tell Mrs Boom to expect you tomorrow,' he said flatly, his tone was one that brooked no argument.

'And I said Sunday,' Rowena repeated, just as firmly.

Sean turned round slowly and moved back into the room until he had reached Rowena, who stood her ground and refused to be intimidated by him. 'I told you once to watch your step,' he said softly. 'I don't often have to repeat myself. When I signed that contract, I became responsible for you. I did not envisage becoming a wife-beater, but I intend to have your respect and obedience no matter what it takes. It's up to you, you can do it the hard way or the easy way, but one way or the other you're going to learn. You might have got away with a lot with your father, but you have me to deal with now. If you don't return tomorrow, and continue to flout my authority, I'll soon show you who's in charge. How do you fancy being persuasively led through the village by your husband back to our connubial home?' he asked softly, but there was a hint of steel in his voice that told Rowena that he meant every word, and she shuddered visibly as the picture of such a spectacle rose before her, and Sean, watching her closely, gave a grim nod. 'You could always put it to the test,' he suggested smoothly, 'because that's exactly what will happen.' The next moment he had left her, and she stood staring in bemused anxiety at the door that he had just closed.

After a moment or two Rowena shook her head bewilderedly. Things had become ridiculous. She had heard what he had said, but she still couldn't believe it. What did it matter where she was, as long as she was well, and had told the persons concerned, like Mrs Broom, so she wouldn't prepare meals for her? She drew in a deep breath. So she hadn't told Sean, and that was a bad mistake, according to him, that was; but Rowena was shocked by his reaction.

She was also deeply worried. Somewhere along the way, they had got their lines crossed, and she had a nasty feeling that he had decided to take her in hand for schooling. Her lips formed into a straight line at the thought. If he hoped to make her a subservient being, then he had another think coming! Beating or no beating, he wouldn't succeed, and what would the village think of their wonderful squire if his wife appeared sporting a black eye—or two black eyes—or any other signs of maltreatment?

She turned away abruptly and walked into the kitchen to make herself a strong cup of coffee, giving herself something to do to take away this new and very unwelcome element that had suddenly erupted into her relationship with Sean, but try as she might, she could not rid herself of Sean's graphic description of the consequential result of her defiance. As for the villagers, they would cheer him all the way, she thought bitterly; she could expect no sympathy there. There would be no sympathy from her father either, who would uphold her new husband's action with his usual old-fashioned North-country bluntness.

There was no help for it, she would have to go back to Tancred House the following morning, she thought disconsolately, as she finished her coffee and rinsed the cup and saucer under the tap and left them on the draining board to dry, then collected Goldie's lead. 'We can't win, Goldie,' she said sadly, as she walked to the door, 'and you're no help,' she scolded gently, 'you might have had the sense to hang on to your temperature!'

When Rowena returned to Tancred House the following morning, she found that the next stall to Goldie's was occupied, although the stall was empty when she and her pet arrived, but the straw and a bucket of water, plus a hay feed tray fixed to the wall of the stall, told its own story. Sean had installed the mare he had mentioned, and Rowena wondered how his new acquisition would take to her howling stable companion, and surmised rather happily that Goldie was bound to unsettle the mare, in which case she might get her wish to have the dog in the house with her.

After lunch, she returned to the stables with Goldie's snack, and hearing no yelping or whines greeting her as she turned the corner to the stables, quickened her steps, because she was afraid that Goldie had somehow managed to get out, and goodness knew where she had gone, she thought anxiously, and if anything had happened to her it would be all on that obnoxious man's head for insisting on keeping her there. Her thoughts raced on as did her feet that carried her inside the stables and towards Goldie's stall, her worried glance only barely resting on the beautiful roan mare that occupied the next stall.

On finding Goldie contentedly sitting in the stall with her head turned towards her stable companion, and her eyes full of curious interest in the stately head of the mare that loomed high above her, almost as if she was mesmerised by the sight of such a large animal at close quarters, Rowena wondered if she was frightened, but there was nothing in her pose to suggest such a fear, only interest.

There was also a familiar smell now about the stables, one that Rowena recognised from her schooldays, when the children had been given riding lessons twice a week at the local stables. It spoke of grooming activities, of rubbing down their mounts after an outing, and the many other tasks to be carried out in the keeping of a horse.

At the sight of Rowena Goldie gave her her usual pleased welcome and ate her snack with unladylike urgency that showed that she was well and truly back to normal.

Now that Rowena could relax, she gave her attention to the mare who from her lofty position had watched Goldie's lapse from grace with what appeared to be a superior look out of her large brown eyes. 'Why, you're beautiful,' Rowena murmured as she reached up to stroke the velvety neck of the mare. 'You must forgive Goldie's manners,' she said softly, 'she's making up for lost time,' she explained, and gave a grin as she envisaged Sean Tancred's haughty reaction to her conversation with his mare had he been privileged to hear it.

The following morning a surprise awaited Rowena when she arrived at the stables, apart from the fact that all was quiet, but this time Rowena was not worried. The arrival of the mare had obviously settled Goldie down, and it looked as if she would have no more worries in that direction, she told herself as she walked towards Goldie's stall, and then stopped in amazement, because the stall was wide open and there was no sign of Goldie.

The mare's stall was also open and empty, but Rowena was not worried about that, Sean had obviously taken her out for an early morning ride, but where was Goldie? One thing was certain, she thought furiously, as she stared around at the empty stable. Goldie could not have got out of that stall, someone had let her out, and there was only one person who could have done that!

Her small lower teeth caught her bottom lip. Had Goldie's yelps unsettled the mare? Was that why Sean had turned her loose, not caring where she went as long as it was away from his precious mare? That did it! When she found Goldie, she would take her away from this place—where, she had no idea, but she wasn't going to risk this happening again.

It was at this point that the sound of horse's hoofs came faintly towards her, and she rushed out of the stables to await the arrival of Sean, her fury building up into a whirlwind that threatened to erupt at the sight of her enemy.

So intense were her feelings that she only had eyes for the tall upright figure of the man she so despised, but as she waited for horse and rider to enter the stabling area, her attention strayed to a rather muddy but thoroughly delighted Goldie dancing along beside horse and rider, with tongue lolling and what Rowena could only describe as a wide grin from ear to ear, as she rushed forward to greet her mistress.

As Rowena fended off the muddy paws of her pet, her eyes met Sean's. There was surprise in hers, for even though she had seen it, she didn't believe it. 'Did she get out?' she asked, unwilling to entertain the thought that he had lowered his haughty standard and actually spared a thought for her pet.

Sean's eyebrows rose as he acknowledged the implication behind her words and chose to ignore it. 'She'll want towelling down,' he said brusquely. 'There's some towels in the cupboard,' he added, indicating the stables. 'She'll make a good dog yet,' he commented casually as he dismounted, 'considering she's had no training.'

Rowena bristled at this last remark, particularly as she had taken a lot of trouble in teaching Goldie to come to heel. Who did he think he was anyway? It was her dog! And she had her own towels, she thought furiously as she led Goldie into the stables and put her in her stall, then closing her in, went to collect her towel from the house.

'Didn't you hear what I said?' Sean demanded, as he led the mare into the stable. 'She wants rubbing down. I'll exercise her, and train her, the rest is your responsibility. You're not at home now,' he added sarcastically.

Rowena gave a gasp of indignation. To hear him talk she had been spoon-fed all her life! It was more than that, of course; he had accused her of trying to get out of her fair share of work. 'I was only going to collect her towel,' she replied icily. 'I have no intention of leaving her in that condition,' she added furiously.

Sean surveyed her through narrowed eyes, then drew in a breath of sheer exasperation. 'I told you where the towels were. There's no sense in traipsing back to the house for one, not even to annoy me. The longer she remains like that, the better the chance of her picking up a real chill,' he added pithily.

Rowena's belligerent stare back at him soon faded as she acknowledged the strength of his argument. Again she was being childish, she thought, but his very attitude made her act out of character and she seemed to be proving his point that she was more concerned with getting back at him than with her pet's health. Without a word she turned back into the stable and going to the old cupboard set against the wall, opened a drawer and took out the first towel that came to hand, then started to work on Goldie.

From the next stall she could hear Sean talking gently to the mare as he rubbed her down. The mare's soft neigh in response to his administrations made her swallow hard. How could he be so horrible to her and yet so understanding with animals? Not, she told herself, that his attitude to her upset her, it didn't, it was just that—She sighed inwardly. What did it matter anyway, they were poles apart and always would be. She got up from her kneeling position and fondled Goldie's ears. 'I'll get your breakfast now,' she said softly, almost in a whisper.

'Make sure there's not too much biscuit in it,' ordered Sean in his lordly manner. 'Plenty of milk, she's still growing. Oh, and make sure she's got plenty of fresh water.'

Rowena gasped. There was nothing wrong with his hearing, she thought vaguely, but she was annoyed. She knew what to feed Goldie and didn't need his autocratic advice. 'Thank you,' she replied acidly. 'I did know that.'

The rest of that week crept by slowly for Rowena. She had ample time on her hands, most of which she spent out on numerous walks with Goldie, in spite of the early runs Sean took her on while exercising his horse, but Goldie was not complaining and seemed to thrive on it.

To Rowena she was only marking time until her father returned, when she intended to bully him into giving her her old job back. She couldn't go on like this. She wasn't living, just existing, and somehow she had to make her father understand and help her out of her boredom.

However, things didn't exactly go as planned. When her father returned, he was a little on the tetchy side, and Rowena surmised astutely that he had not had the roaring welcome he had hoped for from his introduction to Sean's clubs. If only he would wait for people to make their own tentative approach towards him, and get to know them before demanding and expecting their absolute attention on whatever subject he had decided to elaborate upon, he would find companionship. But unfortunately his blunt way of going about things usually had the opposite effect and was more likely to vacate the club room than to populate it.

Rowena's request for work was again turned down adamantly. 'Of course you're bored,' he had said bluntly. 'Join one of those women's things. You're the squire's wife now, and expected to take an interest in the village functions. You won't get anywhere sitting on your own up there. Besides,' he had added, 'it's early days yet. The invitations will roll in, you'll see. Fêtes and things—it's always the squire's wife who hands out the prizes and things. Oh, by the way, tell Sean that I met a colleague of his father's, will you? A Harold Moreton; used to be in shipping, made a fortune apparently, though you wouldn't think it now, gone a bit senile, keeps muttering under his breath,' he added as an afterthought, and that was the end of the talk Rowena had with her father and the end of her hopes of continuing as his secretary.

During the following week, almost as if her father's words had triggered off some action on the home front, Rowena received a letter from the chairman of the village Women's Institute asking her if she would attend the next meeting on the following Wednesday.

Her first thought was that there must have been some mistake. She knew nothing of the village affairs apart from giving the odd hand on the local fête day, and then only doing what was required of her taking over one of the stalls or assisting in the tea tent, but no other contact had been made in the past. It was as her father had so scathingly remarked earlier, that the village people were only after financial help and had no intention of inviting her to join their inner circle.

Not knowing what she should do about it, Rowena decided to approach Sean on the subject, since he was bound to air his views on the matter bluntly, and feeling certain that he would veto any move by the local bigwigs to ensnare her into acting the role of the squire's wife, she was confident that she would be able to refuse the request on some excuse or other.

By this time she knew exactly where he would be during the morning, for the simple reason that Goldie would be with him. She had traitorously transferred her allegiance to the enemy from the morning of her impromptu gallop round the fields with him, and whenever Rowena went to fetch her for her walk, she would first have to locate where Sean was, for Goldie was no longer shut up in the stables during the day, and although Rowena was pleased about this, she couldn't help feeling a little peeved at her dog's defection to the enemy camp.

As Rowena had surmised, Sean was in the makeshift office at the back of the stables going over the plans for the renovation of the house. The following week, the work would be started on what would surely be a long and painstaking operation.

Goldie was sitting by the desk over which Sean was leaning and studying the blueprints spread out before him, and when she saw Rowena she dashed towards her expecting to be taken for a walk. 'Later, Goldie,' said Rowena, as she approached the desk and waited for Sean to acknowledge her presence.

While she waited her eyes travelled over the clean-cut features of the man she still barely knew, even though he was her husband. A strand of his blond hair that grew straight across his forehead had fallen forward, and Rowena knew an absurd wish to brush it back, and the thought horrified her. Was she going soft on him again? she thought distractedly, because if she was, she simply couldn't bear it. Things were bad enough without her adding to her misery.

'Well?' growled Sean, who had glanced up at her and had noted her confusion, which made things worse for her. She quickly thrust the letter at him.

'I—they want me to attend the local W.I. meeting,' she said, adding quickly as she saw his brows go up much as if to query why she was bothering him about it, 'I can't think why. I know nothing about that sort of thing. I thought perhaps you would pass the word on for me,' she ended lamely, hating him for making her flounder; he must know why she had approached him over the matter.

He turned his attention to the letter she had handed him before answering her, then handed it back to her. 'Why not?' he said abruptly. 'You're expected to take an interest in the local community. Accept it. Don't worry about not knowing anything about their activities—Mrs Fisher will put you right there.'

Rowena stared at him. Once again he had let her down, she thought crossly. She had been so sure he would have wanted her to keep out of local affairs. 'I thought you didn't want me——' she began crossly, and flushed as she met his eyes.

'That was on a personal level,' he said slowly

but deliberately, making her want to hit him. 'There's no reason why you shouldn't make yourself useful in other matters.' He gave a casual shrug of his broad shoulders. 'You could refuse, of course, but I should have thought you would welcome the chance of meeting people. It would be better than roaming the woods all day with that hound. She doesn't need the exercise now.'

He need not have said that, Rowena thought furiously, glad to be able to hate him again. Not content with underlining the fact that he wanted her out of his personal life, he had to show her that he knew exactly how she had been filling in her time. Her hand clenched round the letter, crushing it. 'I'll think about it,' she said quietly, and with as much dignity as she could muster left him, with Goldie romping at her side in the hope of a walk.

Rowena did think about it, and she was very tempted to write back and refuse the invitation, but she could not think of a good enough excuse to cover her refusal. There was Sean's advice to consider too, and she knew that if she did turn the invitation down he would be sure to accuse her of self-indulgence apart from a few other well chosen barbs to make her feel uncomfortable.

In the end she accepted the invitation, but made a point of explaining that she knew very little about such matters, making certain that the chairman would not expect her to take a leading role in the proceedings.

The letter she received back from Mrs Fisher thanking her for accepting the invitation told her not to worry about procedure. It was just a friendly meeting that was held once a month to

outline the activities to be carried out and to listen
to any suggestions from the members about any
new and interesting projects they could start up.
She ended by giving Rowena the time of the meeting, and said she hoped that Mrs Tancred would
consider becoming a full member of the Institute.

Mrs Tancred very much doubted that she would
fulfil this hopeful suggestion. It took all sorts to
make a world, but she could not see herself joining
the 'jams and jellies' brigade. They were in a class
of their own. Homemakers, every one of them,
most of them with children, and who needed an
outlet to give them a break from the usual dull
routine of the home.

At least, that was how Rowena saw them, but
she would have been the first to admit that she
could be wrong, for what did she know about an
ordinary housewife's needs? Nothing at all, she
conceded after she had given the matter some
thought.

On attending the meeting, however, she felt that
her earlier surmising on the type of woman who
joined such activities had proved remarkably correct, and her trepidation was somewhat eased by
the sea of friendly homely faces that turned towards her as she walked into the small village hall.

The next minute the stout form of Mrs Fisher
was thrust before her, and she found herself swept
forward towards the platform to join the élite on
the committee. There was no opportunity to make
an objection to this rather V.I.P. treatment, but
Rowena would have much preferred to have sat
with the lesser lights in the stalls.

As she took her place next to the chairman she

felt an intruder and a fraud, and was glad when the meeting commenced after she had received a formal verbal welcome from the chairman.

When she had first entered the hall, it had seemed that the whole village had attended the meeting—all the female population, that was—but as the meeting continued, and discussions were held on either past activities, the regrettable lack of crockery, for instance, at last year's fête, and then it went on to discuss the entertainment requisites for the coming fête, Rowena began to relax and take an interest in the meeting, and was able to look about her, even to the extent of being able to count the number of members present.

There was Mrs Jefferson in the front row, a nice quiet woman with three children, the eldest of whom had just made her a grandmother. Rowena knew her by sight, but the rest of the details had been provided by Miss Heysham. In fact, all Rowena knew about the villagers had at one time or another been passed on by the schoolteacher, who had taken a kindly interest in her children's parents.

In all there were about sixteen members seated in the hall, and four committee members on the platform. Hardly a crowd, but they had appeared twice as many to the apprehensive Rowena.

There were of course several members that Rowena did not know, and they were younger than the majority, and took a more lively interest in the proceedings with bright suggestions for livening up the entertainment side of the forthcoming fête, all of which were effectively sidetracked by the redoubtable Mrs Fisher, ably assisted by her committee, who was obviously a force, if not the force to be reckoned with if changes were to be wrought in what was an age-old constitution—the village fête.

As Rowena took silent note of the battle between what she would have described as the 'Mods' and the 'Conservatives', she decided it was a very one-sided affair, for all the 'Conservatives' were unfortunately on the platform and held seniority over their younger compatriots. She also gained the distinct impression that the group was hardly a united one, and that the village fête was not the only subject they disagreed upon.

So the meeting proceeded, and Rowena became intrigued by the machinations of the village ladies, who were now discussing various ways of contributing to a national fund raising scheme, although she would not have thought that patchwork quilts were quite the thing to send to far-distant Asian communities in dire need of nutrition, and judging by the vociferous response this suggestion received from the Mods, she was not alone in this, but on this occasion they won the day, with a tight-lipped Mrs Fisher acknowledging defeat and adopting the much more sensible suggestion of collecting monetary aid to be sent to the appeal.

As Rowena listened but took no part in the discussions, for she would have been horribly embarrassed if she had been used as a mediator between the forces, having to throw her weight in to settle the issue, she could not help reverting to the engagement party, and the sylph-like form of Diana Fisher, and found it hard to reconcile the fact that this lady of large proportions and even larger voice that boomed across the room with the power of a foghorn was Diana's mother, and she couldn't help wondering how Sean would have got on with his mother-in-law, if things had been different.

As this thought occurred to her, so did another one. There was no doubting the fact that Mrs Fisher and her four aides ruled supreme in the village affairs, and had done so for many years. In asking Rowena to join the Institute, Mrs Fisher was only making a polite gesture towards the squire's wife, and that was all. Rowena was not expected to take any real interest in the Institute, but only to attend in her capacity as Sean's wife.

She might as well have been a dummy, she thought ironically, and wondered what the intimidating Mrs Fisher would have done if she had cheered on the 'Mods' as she had at times been tempted to do!

It all echoed her new and highly unsatisfactory position in village affairs, she thought miserably, and she ought to have stuck to her guns and turned the invitation down. She had no desire to thrust herself upon the community—not that it would have made any difference if she had, as the outcome would have been the same, but at least Rowena had known what to expect. She was an outsider, and always would be; lip-service only would be paid to her, but the genuine hand of friendship would not be offered, she thought sadly, as she left the hall after the meeting, with Mrs Fisher seeing her to the door and voicing her thanks for her attendance.

Sean had known how it would be, she thought,

as she made her way back to Tancred House. Not that he would have thought to warn her not to expect too much if she had hoped to make an impression in such circles. Instead he had deliberately encouraged her to take an interest in the village life, although he had known full well that she would be attempting to climb an insurmountable barrier, and the thought must have given him a great deal of pleasure.

CHAPTER SEVEN

ROWENA might have been right about a few of the leading lights of the village's intention as to her involvement in local affairs, but to her surprise, this feeling was only shared by a few people.

It was true that those few people, namely Mrs Fisher, Mrs Dean, the garrulous Miss James, who ran the small village post office, and a Mrs Finton, a small mousey woman, and cousin of Mrs Fisher, who completely dominated her, reigned supreme in the role of organisers for all of the activities in the small village—activities, that was, that concerned group involvements. But there were other involvements in the running of certain aspects of welfare, and it was not long before Rowena found herself caught up with these.

It all started with an invitation from the vicar's wife, a Mrs Marsden, a tall, thin woman in her seventies, whom Rowena had met after her wedding to Sean, and who had seemed to be a little on the vague side. But as Rowena took afternoon tea with her that day, she saw another side to the kindly woman and felt an affinity towards her.

It was not so much what she said as what she left out when touching upon local affairs. 'I'm afraid I haven't taken as much interest in the village affairs as perhaps a vicar's wife is expected to do,' she began apologetically. 'My hobbyhorse is the young people of the village,' she went on, 'and I did feel that perhaps they were being left out.' She looked up at Rowena quickly, as if not certain whether to go on, then having decided to go ahead, continued. 'For instance, I've felt for some time that we really ought to start up another Brownie pack in the village. We have a Scout group, run by Mr Collyer, you know,' she told Rowena, 'but sadly they're in dire need of new premises. They used to share the village hall, which is, of course, the church hall with the Women's Institute, but it's only a local affair and has no affiliation with what we know as a W.I.' She gave Rowena a quick conspiratorial look. 'But I'm afraid things have not gone at all smoothly there. Unfortunately Mr Collyer has got on the wrong side of Mrs Fisher, who always finds reasons why the Scout group can't have the hall on specified days. In order to keep the movement going, and to avoid further confrontation with the W.I., Mr Collyer now holds the meetings at his home, but it's very awkward for him.'

She gave Rowena a smile. 'I expect you're wondering what this has to do with you, aren't you?' she said. 'But you see I'm hoping that you'll take

an interest in the young folk.' She gave Rowena
another smile as she added, 'We're not so young as
we were, and I'm hoping that the vicar will decide
to retire this coming year, and if so, I do want to
make sure that there'll be someone who'll see to
their needs. Sean did say that he hoped to be able
to provide another hall for the village—the old
blacksmith's place has been empty for years and as
it's right in the centre of the village, it will make an
excellent site for the new hall. I know Sean is very
busy, indeed he'll be busy for a long time, and I
don't feel it would be fair to worry him over such
details at this point in time—so I thought I would
have a word with you.'

Rowena was not quite sure what was expected
of her, and started to point this out. 'I'm not
sure——' she began, but was interrupted gently by
Mrs Marsden.

'I'm not very good at explaining anything,' she
said with another smile. 'What I'm trying to say is,
will you please keep a watchful eye out for the
younger children? Their needs have had to take a
back seat lately,' she gave a small grimace, 'well,
for quite some time, in fact, and there hasn't been
much that I could do about it,' she gave a shrug of
her thin shoulders, 'not with only one village hall.
Now things are changing, but I'm afraid we must
be vigilant or we shall find that another use will be
put to the new hall. It will be much bigger than the
church hall, and I've heard rumours of the Institute intending to use it for bring-and-buy sales, all
for a worthy cause, I'm sure, but before we know
where we are, other uses as well, anything in fact
but what it was originally intended for.' She gave

Rowena a searching look. 'I need an ally,' she said quietly, 'and who better than the squire's wife?' she ended brightly.

Rowena tried to look gratified and hoped her expression did not give her thoughts away. How could she explain how things were between her and Sean? That he would no more listen to any suggestion of hers than he would abandon the estate.

In all probability, he would go out of his way to make any such project awkward, simply because she had dared to get involved. She swallowed. Of all the people to ask for help, Mrs Marsden had unwittingly picked on the one person who could not help her, although Rowena did not see how she could tell her this without causing both of them a great deal of embarrassment—not so much for her as for the vicar's wife, for it was patently obvious that she had no idea of the true state of the marriage or the reason why it had taken place. She had admitted that she had not taken a great deal of interest in the local social functions, and in this she was like Jenny Heysham, although she had been worried over Rowena's sudden decision to marry Sean.

Neither of these two kindly women would waste their time in idle gossip, and would be sure to send the scandalmongers on their way with a few well chosen words of reproof.

Rowena knew she had to say something and it had to sound helpful, even though there would be little real chance of success in her fulfilling the role Mrs Marsden had outlined. 'Of course I'll help in whatever way I can,' she said as brightly as she was able, since it was the truth. She would try, in spite of the overwhelming odds against success.

The answer pleased the vicar's wife, who positively beamed at her. 'Now that's what I'd hoped you would say,' she replied, 'and we shall have to get down to a plan of campaign later. It's early days yet. I mean, you haven't really had time to settle down to married life yet, have you? and with Sean so busy——' She shook her head sadly. 'He's had such a hard time of it trying to keep things going on a pittance. I really think they ought to do something about death duties, you know, particularly when it's an old estate.' She broke off suddenly, and gave Rowena's arm, that was lying on the arm of her chair next to her, a pat. 'Well, thanks to your father he has no more worries on that score. I thought he looked more relaxed at the wedding than he'd looked for years. But then I don't have to tell you that, do I? I'm so happy for you both. Sean is a good man and has done much for his people.'

It all depended, Rowena thought sourly, on which side of the fence you were standing, and she was definitely on the other side!

After she had left Mrs Marsden, with a promise to attend a sewing evening at the vicarage on the following Wednesday, she wondered how long it would take for the vicar's wife to realise just how little influence Rowena had over the proud squire of the village, and her thoughts were not peaceful ones as she walked into Tancred House.

The same went for Jenny Heysham, she thought miserably, for although she was not one to listen to gossip, Rowena knew there was little that escaped her attention, and sooner or later she was bound to know the truth. For the sake of her pride, Rowena was prepared to let her go on thinking as everybody else did, that she had grabbed at the chance of marrying the handsome squire using her father's money as bait to gain her objective—and that was bad enough, but if her mother's old friend should discover the real motive behind the marriage, she would be not only shocked, but very distressed.

As things stood, she would feel immensely sorry for Rowena once she had heard that although she had married Sean Tancred, she was his wife in name only, and that Rowena had failed to gain his affection, risking all on a childish dream that was never to be fulfilled.

That sort of sympathy Rowena could put up with—she was receiving it every day from Mrs Broom, and probably from some of the villagers, apart from the ones who thought it served her right for trying to gatecrash her way into society— as Sean thought, and were only too ready to point the finger of scorn her way, and actually enjoy her discomfiture.

Rowena was too engrossed with her thoughts to notice Sean standing by the staircase, and did not see him until she was about to go up the stairs. Her instant scowl at the sight of him caused him some amusement, but he said nothing of this to her and held out a letter towards her. 'I believe this is yours,' he commented dryly. 'You might ask that brother of yours to try and write a little more legibly in the future,' and with that he left her.

As Rowena looked at the letter that Sean had

given her she recognised David's writing, or rather
scrawl, and wondered vaguely how it had got de-
livered in the first place. His writing had never
been good, but since he had become involved in
the art world it had got decidedly worse, she
thought, and surely it should have got better.

Considering how much he hated writing, she
ought to be grateful that he had made the effort,
she told herself as she went on up to her room.

After taking off her jacket, she settled down to
read the letter and find out what David's reaction
to the marriage had been, but as she turned the
letter to open it, her eyes widened when she saw
that it had already been opened.

So that was what Sean had meant when he had
sarcastically requested that she ask her brother to
write more clearly! He had opened the letter by
mistake! She turned the letter back to the front
again and had to admit that the 'Mrs' could well
have been taken for 'Mr', and it would never have
occurred to His Lofty Highness that the letter belonged to her.

With a sigh of exasperation, Rowena took the
letter from the envelope and deciphered David's
message.

It was more or less as she had expected, the first
part anyway. The shock was there, and his blunt,
'I thought you had got over him years ago,' made
her teeth clench on her lower lip. There was more
to come, and with the ghastly thought that Sean
might have read the letter, she could cheerfully
have murdered him. 'Apparently it went deeper
than we had realised,' he went on blithely. 'You
should have a medal for perseverance, and you
have my congratulations on landing your man!'

He had gone on to say that he hoped to be able to get home for a weekend at the start of the summer vacation, and after that he was off to Paris with a party on a sketching holiday.

Rowena's hand shook as she put the letter down. 'Thanks, pal,' she commented bitterly, and stared with unseeing eyes at the deep-piled carpet at her feet.

The chance that Sean had not read the letter was too small to be considered. Rowena was certain that he had, and wondered miserably why fate was ganging up on her in this way, and couldn't think why this should happen to her. As far as she had known, she had led an uneventful life and done nothing to incur the wrath of the powers that be. But here she was, forced to live a lie with a man she heartily disliked, and as if that wasn't enough, deserted by her only ally in the house, her dog, who had not only ingratiated herself with Sean, but with the housekeeper as well, for when Sean had gone off on one of his inspections of the estate, and had not wanted Goldie with him, she would invariably make her way to the kitchen and the company of Mrs Broom, plus any titbits that were going.

Rowena shook her head slowly. She had enough to worry about without dwelling on Goldie's defection. She really had no complaint in that direction, as Goldie had proved that she was a born survivor. Her worry was with David and his forthcoming visit in about three months' time.

Hearing the rattle of crockery coming from the dining room, Rowena got up quickly and went to the hatch, and there was her tea tray. 'I sent it up earlier,' Mrs Broom called up after Rowena had taken the tray out of the hatch. 'Mr Sean said you were out.'

'I'm sorry,' Rowena replied apologetically, 'I should have told you.'

'No bother,' was Mrs Broom's calm answer,' I was making a pot of tea anyway.'

Rowena thanked her, then took the tea tray in to her sitting-room and poured herself a cup of tea. She ought to have remembered to tell Mrs Broom that she was having tea out, she thought ruefully, and wondered if she would ever get used to having to leave an itinerary of her movements each time she went anywhere, and the sad fact was that she would have to.

Her eye then caught David's letter that she had left on the sofa, and slowly travelled round the room. What would he think of her new living quarters, she asked herself ironically, and the way she had been isolated from the family apartments like a pensioned-off nanny who had to be taken care of?

The hand holding the tea-cup shook and a few drops of tea spilled on to her skirt. She could not let him come—not without telling him the truth—and where would that leave him? If he should ever find out the true reason for her marriage, he would feel responsible for what had happened, and knowing him, he would do something about it—what, Rowena had no idea, apart from demanding that Rowena put an end to what he would describe as a farce, after he had verbally attacked Sean for his treatment of his sister, and it might not stop at a verbal lashing either, she thought miserably, knowing David's quick temper.

Not that that would be the end of it, Rowena told herself with a quick intake of breath on an insight into the future reverberations from such a confrontation. He was going to feel bad enough about things as it was, but when he learnt of the conditions that bound both Sean and her father to the contract, he would feel even worse, for he would see that there was nothing that he could do about it—not without ruining his father, and like Rowena, even though he did not see eye to eye with him, it was hardly likely that he would want to ruin him.

Rowena drank her tea, then took the tray out to the hatch and sent it back to the kitchen, calling out a 'Thank you,' to Mrs Broom as she did so, and again David came to mind as she thought of his reactions to this part of the bargain that her father had so thoughtlessly arranged for her, and that made her feel as if she had some contagious disease that necessitated such an arrangement.

'Stop it!' she whispered fiercely to herself. 'This sort of thinking is getting you nowhere! Try thinking constructively.' There must be a way of preventing David from learning the truth, she told herself sternly, and put her mind to the task.

After a few moments' thought, however, she gave a deep sigh. Apart from actually having a contagious disease, she could come up with no solution that would explain her unusual living arrangements.

Three months left her plenty of room for scope and she was going to need all that time to work something out, she thought ironically. She might just be lucky and catch mumps; it was the only childish ailment that she knew that she had not had, and neither had David. It could be a very painful complaint to catch, particularly in an older person, and nasty enough to make David agree to give her a wide berth during his visit home. It would be up to Sean then to entertain his brother-in-law, and Rowena no more enjoyed envisaging that prospect than she enjoyed the thought of David finding out the truth.

As she had promised to attend Mrs Marsden's sewing circle the following Wednesday, she was duty bound to keep that promise, but she fervently wished that she had been able to find some excuse for not attending. She liked Mrs Marsden, but was again apprehensive about the other members of the circle and expected to find herself sitting next to the indomitable Mrs Fisher, for she could not imagine a single function in the village that would take place— or even dare to take place without her presence or indeed her approval.

On arrival at the vicarage, however, she found that the sewing circle consisted of the younger members of the community, and was a little dismayed to find Diana Fisher and Lucinda Dean among them, acting as Mrs Marsden's aides, as the rest of the circle consisted of children between the ages of fourteen and sixteen.

'Diana and Lucinda ably assist me in our little activities,' Mrs Marsden said cheerfully, as she ushered Rowena in to the vicarage lounge. 'Lucinda is the one who gives us all the know-how in the embroidery class, and is exceptionally clever with the needle, although she doesn't like my saying so,' she went on with a smile at the embarrassed-looking Lucinda, who immediately bent down to check on one of the girls' stitches, 'and Diana comes to help organise things,' went on Mrs Marsden, happily ignorant of the fact that neither Diana nor Lucinda had appeared in any way enthusiastic over the vicar's wife's latest recruit to the ranks.

It was hardly likely that they would show any enthusiasm, Rowena thought unhappily. She would get as much assistance from them as she had received from their parents, for although she was not sure about Lucinda's feelings where Sean was concerned, she was sure about Diana's and that his marriage must have been a terrible blow to her, and she was not likely to welcome the girl who had bought her way into Sean Tancred's life.

As the evening progressed, it looked to all intent and purpose as if all was well. Diana was polite to Rowena and so was Lucinda, but Rowena was very much aware of the undercurrents that flowed between them and once again she was back in the bedroom of Tancred House as a young impressionable girl and listening to Diana and Lucinda's blunt remarks.

It was impossible, she thought wretchedly, for her to live down the past. No one was going to let her ever forget that she had once had a bad crush on Sean, and no one would believe her if she told them that she had long since grown out of it. How could they, when she had married the wretched man? she asked herself bitterly.

By the time they were half-way through the evening Rowena had promised herself that she would find some excuse for bowing out of any further involvement in the sewing class, or any other activity that Mrs Marsden wished to include her in. There had been several projects mentioned, a nature ramble, a basket weaving class, the vicar's wife was not short of ideas, just helpers, apparently, but Rowena was determined to keep her distance. She knew she was not wanted by Diana or Lucinda, and as their mothers ruled supreme in the adult activities, their daughters had taken the same role in the children's activities. Had Rowena been the ambitious, pushing type that they all thought she was, then she would have gone ahead regardless, but she was sure that if she persisted in joining in their activities it would not be long before Diana and Lucinda found an excuse to drop out, leaving Mrs Marsden without their very useful contributions to her pet projects.

During the weeks that followed, Rowena was to find that the gentle vicar's wife became a positive terrier in hunting out her quarry, in this case, the squire's wife! As Rowena's excuses became thinner over her reasons for not going on whatever excursion was planned, so Mrs Marsden's determination grew, and Rowena wondered if she did have some inkling of how matters stood with her and Diana and Lucinda, and if so, she seemed bent on overcoming their differences, and although nothing had been said, Rowena was certain that she had her welfare in mind, and refused to let her be pushed out of circulation.

Things had changed at Tancred House too. Sean had engaged a manager for the estate, to leave him free to watch over the repairs now being carried out in the house, and it seemed that wherever Rowena went she ran into him.

They had now reached a passive acceptance of each other's presence, passive but still wary, on Rowena's part anyway, for she was still treated as an intruder who had to be put up with as a necessary evil, and his attitude when he spoke to her clearly showed this.

A fortnight after the estate manager began work, Sean called on Rowena to help out with some secretarial work in the estate office. 'John's got his hands full at the moment with the outside work,' he told her, 'and is slogging away at the typewriter in the evenings to catch up. You might as well make yourself useful by seeing to that part for him. You've nothing else on, have you?' he demanded autocratically, almost daring her to refuse.

Rowena bit back the urge to be awkward and refuse. She needed the work, and it was stupid to be churlish. She said nothing, but just nodded her acceptance and left him before he could say anything else. The less conversation she had with him the better her chance of survival.

CHAPTER EIGHT

ALTHOUGH Rowena's help in the estate office was to be on a purely occasional basis, when something needed to be catalogued, or the odd letter sent to the Ministry of Agriculture, she was soon fully immersed in the work, and spent most mornings there, after John Apsley, a bright young graduate from agriculture college, had got over the fact that his 'typist' was his boss's wife, and had stopped apologising to her each time he pushed work her way.

Once this awkward phase was over, it was not long before he was discussing the work with her, and his views on modern farming methods. 'They didn't exactly go down well with old Mr Stokes,' he told Rowena one morning after his estate rounds. 'You know that farm is the largest on the estate yet has the poorest returns. The machinery has to be seen to be believed, and only old Stokes knows how to get it going. If I so much as hint that it's time that it was on the scrap-heap, he does a war dance,' he said with a grin, then he was serious again. 'I was wondering,' he said carefully, 'if you would have a word with Mr Tancred. I understand that Stokes is retiring in about two months' time. I shall have to find another tenant to run the farm, but I can't see any aspiring would-be farmer taking it on—not with such ancient machinery to work with. The machinery must be replaced some time, and the sooner the better. Trouble is,' he went on slowly, 'the cost's going to be a bit on the hefty side. I'd say everything wants replacing, plus a harvester. Of course,' he added hastily, 'some things can wait a while until the farm is paying for itself.'

It seemed to Rowena that whatever she did she ran into snags. She really enjoyed the work in the office, and had learnt a great deal about estate management affairs, but it looked as if her peace was at an end, for if she agreed to tackle Sean about this matter, she knew he would accuse her of interference in his affairs, and if she was successful, which was hardly likely, but had to be considered, this would not be the only matter in which John would seek her co-operation. 'I think it would be better if you were to have a word with him,' she said quietly. 'I mean, you could go into details, couldn't you? He's bound to want facts and things on paper,' she added lamely.

'Oh, I can get the figures out,' John assured her, happily ignorant of her despondency. 'He more or less knows the farm's losing money and I suppose it must have been awkward for him coping with old Stokes. I understood from the old man's mutterings that his family had been tenants there from the year dot, and he would have none of those new-fangled motors around the place. I can also show him what returns are likely if the farm is modernised,' he added eagerly.

After this, there was nothing Rowena could say, and she had to accept the task of putting the proposition to Sean. If anyone else had been working with him, he could hardly have asked them to do it, and would have had to have a word with Sean himself. It was sadly obvious that John knew nothing of the unusual conditions of her marriage. As a newcomer to the village, he would probably hear in time, but Rowena could hardly enlighten him herself.

Sean's reaction was just as she had known it would be when she put it to him the following morning before going to the office. 'I asked you to help out,' he said sarcastically, 'not take over the manager's affairs. Missing the big time, are you? I

heard you were your father's right hand in the
City,' he added jeeringly. 'Well, we can manage as
we are,' he grated, and thrust the papers that
Rowena had given him to study back at her without so much as glancing at them.

She took a deep breath, and wondered why she
bothered. She had known what the outcome would
be, and wanted to fling the papers back at him,
but managed to restrain herself. 'I have nothing to
do with it,' she got out quietly. 'This is Mr
Apsley's work. He just wants you to study his
report and give him some indication of whether
you agree to his recommendations over Home
Farm.'

'Then why the devil didn't he approach me himself?' snarled Sean, and snatched the papers back
from Rowena and ran his eyes down the print,
then raised his eyebrows. 'Does he realise how
much this is going to cost?' he demanded. 'I'm not
made of money.' His caustic eyes then rested on
Rowena, who was watching a workman ascending
a ladder outside the house, completely detaching
herself from any of his remarks. 'I suppose we
could ask dear old Dad to cough up an extra few
thousand, couldn't we?' he taunted.

Rowena's eyes left the man on the ladder and
rested on Sean. The dislike she felt for him was
plainly visible in her brown eyes. 'I see no reason
why not,' she replied steadily. 'He would see it as
an investment.'

Sean's eyes narrowed at her reply. 'But they
don't all come off, do they?' he said softly.

Rowena blinked as she caught the implication
behind his words. 'As a matter of fact they usually
do,' she got out stiffly, 'but you must allow him

one blind spot in his brilliant career.'

She heard Sean's swift intake of breath as she turned away sharply and the next moment found her wrist caught in a grip of steel and she was propelled back towards him, her slight body hard up against his. 'I don't care for your tone, Mrs Tancred,' he said softly, his grip tightening on her slim wrist.

'That makes two of us,' Rowena got out breathlessly, for the sudden movement had shocked her. 'Would you please let go of my wrist?' she demanded furiously. 'Before that man falls off that ladder staring at us!' she added, directing Sean's attention to the workman who looked in a precarious position as he peered over at them.

'He probably thinks it's a love scene,' Sean replied mockingly, his grip still holding her close to him. 'We never got round to a honeymoon, did we?' he taunted softly.

Rowena chose to ignore this taunt. 'If that's what he thinks, then he deserves to fall on his head!' she bit out.

Then he released her as suddenly as he had caught her to him, and his low chuckle followed Rowena as she marched off to the office with her head held high and her cheeks tinted a delicate pink.

After this unwarranted attack on her, she made a point of keeping her distance from Sean. If John Apsley wanted any more help from her outside of her office duties, then he was going to be unlucky, she told herself firmly.

It was not so much the verbal lashings as the manhandling part of their last encounter that most worried her. She had sensed Sean's satisfaction at actually causing her physical discomfort, and she knew he would adopt this method of imposing his authority on her whenever an opportunity presented itself. It was this aspect of their relationship that threw her into utter despondency.

That she despised him was a plain fact, but even despising him, she had felt an attraction towards him, and this had really frightened her. He could call her what he liked as long as he kept his hands off her, and almost frantically Rowena decided never again to openly show her feelings towards him.

A change of attitude was badly needed, and no matter how it hurt, she had to alter her approach from an antagonistic one to a servile one, and knew instinctively that he would hate that. He would hate it so much that he would go out of his way to avoid her, she thought with a sudden flash of intuition, and began to feel better about things, wondering why she hadn't thought of that before.

So another week passed, and Rowena busied herself in her work, quietly awaiting the chance of presenting her new image to Sean, and was actually disappointed when no opportunity presented itself. John had now got the go-ahead over the modernisation of the farm and had buried himself under a welter of facts and figures and had enough to occupy himself with for some time to come.

As Mrs Marsden had won the last round in the battle, and had extracted a promise from Rowena to go to the sewing circle the following week, Rowena duly went.

The evening turned out to be a more interesting one than the previous one, in that a newcomer to the village was introduced to the assembly by the vicar, who walked in on them accompanied by a tall, thin, and rather ascetic-looking fair man in his late twenties. 'This, Peter, is our little Wednesday evening gathering,' he said jovially. 'Of course, you'll meet everyone at the hall tomorrow evening, but here are a few of our stalwart helpers.'

Rowena cast a quick glance towards the vicar's wife. So that was why she had insisted upon Rowena's presence, although she could hardly be called a 'stalwart helper'—more of a 'stalwart dodger,' she thought dryly.

'Ah, Mrs Tancred,' said the vicar, and walked over to her. 'This is my new curate, Peter Roshier,' he said, introducing the young man by his side. 'Mrs Tancred is our worthy squire's wife,' he explained, and looked back at Rowena. 'I'm hoping to call on him tomorrow about eleven. I suppose he could spare a quarter of an hour or so?' he asked her.

Rowena replied that she would mention this to her husband, and could feel Diana's eyes upon her as she said this and was glad when the conversation turned to other matters.

In spite of her new resolution to change her attitude towards Sean, when it came to the test, Rowena's courage failed her and she left Mrs Broom a note to give to him advising him of the vicar's visit that morning, and the new curate he was bringing with him.

This way of communicating with him would

probably infuriate him, she thought, but he had only himself to blame, and to prove her point she had only to show him her wrist that still showed where he had gripped her, although the marks were much fainter now than they had been.

By the time another fortnight had passed Rowena found herself having to divide her time between the office duties and community affairs.

There was no need now for Mrs Marsden to hound her out of her solitude, as the advent of the curate's arrival had brought about a climatic change in Rowena's relationship with Diana and Lucinda, and in Lucinda's case the change could almost be called dramatic.

It did not take Rowena long to see that Peter Roshier was a marked man, and that under the cover of a studious vagueness he was very shy, and she wondered how long it would take him to realise that Lucinda had him firmly fixed in her sights.

Lucinda now dressed with care. She no longer wore the old but comfortable corduroy trousers and cotton tops, whichever was nearest to hand, for no thought had previously gone into her appearance. Her hair too was now carefully curled, and the whole effect presented the village with an entirely new picture of the girl they had once known.

As Lucinda's appearance had altered, so had her feelings towards her childhood friend, Diana. Rowena had never been certain just how close they had been, but the sad fact was that, as in the wild, a tigress hunts alone. Not that Rowena blamed her; Diana's presence would be seen as a definite handicap in the hunt. Her looks alone presented a hurdle Lucinda would have to overcome in order to gain her objective.

To Rowena's consternation, she found herself brought into the fray, not as a silent onlooker but as an ally, not only to Lucinda but to Peter as well, for quite different reasons.

In both cases the reasoning behind the moves were sound, and in dismay Rowena could see this. From Lucinda's point of view, Rowena was not a rival, although there must have been times when she had a few worries on this point.

Peter Roshier's case, however, was more complex, and much more difficult for Rowena, because it was in direct opposition to Lucinda's hopes.

In a way, Rowena blamed Sean for placing her in this difficult position, since it was through him that she had got on a closer acquaintance with Peter. It all started after the vicar had called on Sean, and had received an invitation to take a glass of sherry with Sean that evening, and naturally the invitation included his new curate.

To her amazement Rowena had received an order from Sean to join in this small gathering, and however much she wanted to refuse, she knew she would have to comply, although the reason why he wanted her there was beyond her.

The evening had loomed on her horizon like a cloud that heralded heavy weather ahead, and Sean's sarcastic remark that here was her chance to shine as the squire's wife did nothing to alleviate her worry.

To her surprise Rowena really enjoyed the evening, and as the possibility of her even remotely enjoying herself had never occurred to her, the pleasure was all the more appreciated.

The role of hostess was not new to her. Her father's entertaining had given her plenty of practice, and with her natural flair for putting newcomers at ease, it was not long before she was holding an animated conversation with Peter Roshier, and had forgotten to watch for Sean's caustic glance her way, reminding her that she was only there on sufferance and the little grocer's daughter should be seen but not heard!

In many ways, Peter reminded Rowena of David. He had the same fresh, almost innocent outlook on life that only a blatant injustice would rouse to action. He was not really at home in social gatherings, but was prepared to put up with them as part of his duties as a cleric, but he would be more at ease carrying out the positive side of his calling.

Rowena liked him very much, and found herself wanting to adopt a protective attitude towards him, much as she had done with her brother, although at that time of their acquaintance no such role was called for.

By the end of the evening they were firm friends, and the vicar, having drawn Sean aside for a private word with him regarding his forthcoming retirement, nodded his approval at this state of affairs, for Peter was a distant relative of his, and he sought Sean's permission to grant the living of the parish to Peter after his retirement.

Rowena was really sorry when the evening ended. It had been like old times to her, and although she had not really missed the social side of her life, she had certainly missed David's company, and as she watched the vicar and Peter depart, she felt a great void of loneliness envelop her, and had to blink hard to stem the tears that welled up in her eyes.

'It appears that I shall have to give a few more sherry evenings to introduce the new curate,' Sean said, breaking into Rowena's unhappy musings, and it took a second or two for her to realise that he was addressing her, and in what sounded like a conciliatory way and she turned her gaze from the window back to him. 'It appears that you are an excellent hostess,' he went on musingly, and as Rowena's eyes widened at what might be interpreted as a compliment, he added indifferently, 'Still, I suppose you've had plenty of practice entertaining those City tycoons. Country parsons must be a bore for you, although Roshier seemed satisfied with the attention you gave him.'

Rowena drew in a deep breath. If she didn't know Sean better she might have thought he was put out by her attention to Peter, but she knew better. He just wanted to spoil her evening, and recalling her earlier decision not to oppose him, she managed a bright smile. 'As you said, I've been well trained,' she replied quietly. 'We Southalls always give value for money,' she added softly, and walked to the door.

'Going already?' taunted Sean. 'I rather thought we might make an evening of it. I shall have to arrange a few get-togethers for us. I don't seem to see much of you these days, do I? I have an odd feeling that you're avoiding me, handing Mrs

Broom notes to give to me, for instance.'

Rowena sighed inwardly. She thought she wouldn't get away with that. 'I just thought it would be quicker,' she replied steadily. 'Mrs Broom would see you at breakfast and there wasn't much time—or there wouldn't have been, by the time I'd found you. You could have been anywhere,' she added firmly.

'Then perhaps we ought to have breakfast together,' Sean said softly. 'Is that what you'd like? Perhaps supper too,' he taunted.

Rowena's horrified, 'No!' rushed out before she realised, and she felt her cheeks grow pink under Sean's steady gaze. 'I mean, I'm quite happy with the present arrangements,' she almost babbled in her panic at the thought of finding herself constantly alone in his company.

Sean continued to look at her, and during the heavy silence that followed Rowena wished miserably that she could just walk out on him, but she knew he hadn't finished tormenting her. 'Are you afraid of me?' he demanded with a hint of surprise in his voice, as if the thought had just occurred to him.

How on earth could she answer that? Rowena thought as she stared back at him. If he wanted the truth it was yes; she was afraid of what he could do to her emotions. Afraid of her reaction, because she was still attracted to him in spite of everything. 'Of course not!' she managed to get out indignantly.

'I'm almost inclined to put that to the test,' Sean said softly, his blue eyes searing into Rowena's startled brown ones. 'I don't believe you. However, we shall see. I've decided to give a ball in aid of church funds,' he announced grandly, giving Rowena's thumping heart a chance to slow down. 'I gather from the vicar that the bells need replacing. We haven't had a hunt ball for years, so I shall combine the two.' He gave Rowena a slow appraisal that started her heart thumping again. 'I shall expect a lot of help from you,' he said, 'organising it. I'm a bit hampered at the moment with the restoration plans, so a lot of the arrangements will be left for you to see to.' He stared out of the drawing-room window to the gathering darkness beyond. 'Three weeks should be ample time to get it organised,' then he looked back quickly at the apprehensive Rowena. 'I shall also expect to be consulted on the arrangements, all along the way,' he added meaningfully. 'I shall not take kindly to any future notes being handed to me by Mrs Broom—do I make myself clear?' he demanded haughtily.

Rowena swallowed, then gave an abrupt nod. Sean had made himself abundantly clear—clear enough for her to be under no illusion as to the real purpose behind the exercise. He wanted to put his theory that she was afraid of him to the test, and what better way of doing it than to force her into his company, she thought miserably, as she thought of the numerous occasions on which she would have to seek him out in order to keep him in touch with things. She would also need his advice, she thought wretchedly. She knew nothing about hunt balls, and who should be invited, 'I know nothing about hunt balls,' she said breathlessly, hoping that he would assign the task to someone else.

'But I do,' Sean said softly, 'so you'll have to come to me, won't you?'

Rowena looked quickly away from the mocking light in his eyes, hating him for making his reply sound more like an amorous suggestion than the cold ultimatum it really was. 'Very well,' she replied stiffly, and before he could enlarge on this theme she turned on her heel and left him.

In the days that followed, Rowena was often to look back on her early days at Tancred House, and how she had wondered how she was going to fill in her time, for now it seemed that there were not enough hours in a day to complete all she had to get through.

As Sean had threatened, for that was how Rowena had seen his directions concerning the arrangements for the ball, not a day went by without her having to seek him out, and on one or two occasions in the evening, and this she tried to avoid, since she was sure that he would take it as an encroachment on his private life, but in view of the time limit and the fact that the queries could not wait, she had no choice. To her surprise, however, he accepted her presence with companionable ease, so much so that Rowena was in danger of being lulled into a fool's paradise, but she was too sensible a person to linger long under any such pretensions. Whenever she did find herself looking at him as he was giving her advice, and, starting to wander into the land of happy endings, she would pull herself together, allowing herself no leeway and reminding herself with punitive clarity of Sean's earlier remarks on her position at Tancred House.

Only when she was in her rooms at the end of the day did she allow herself the luxury of truth, and that she had once again fallen under the spell of the autocratic owner of the house she now lived in.

These were dangerous admissions, this she knew, but she was powerless to stop them invading her thoughts, though it was a blessed relief to let them roam free of the iron hold she was forced to keep herself on during the day, and her numerous encounters with the man who despised her in spite of his assumed goodwill towards her merely to gain his objective. He had hated to think he had been wrong in his earlier assessment of her feelings where he had been concerned, and he meant to ascertain the truth. Of this Rowena was in no doubt, for underneath his smooth comments she had sensed his probing into her finer senses.

It was akin to a battle of wits, she thought sadly. She had always to be on her guard, and she looked forward to the day of the ball with fervent eagerness, not with anticipation at the culmination of all her efforts, but because she could then relapse to her nondescript role.

During this period she had somehow found time to join in a few of Mrs Marsden's little evenings, and on one occasion a ramble on a Sunday afternoon, when she found Peter keeping in close proximity. Because she liked him so much, and they hit it off so well, it had never occurred to her that others might take an exception to their close friendship, and the fact that Peter had made a point of seeing her home whenever she went to an evening circle did not go unnoticed either, in spite of her smiling protests that she had not far to go, and it had taken a little while for her to catch on to his insistence on this point, and she then wondered why she had been so slow.

It had been the vicar's habit to appear at the end of the evening, when tea would be handed round to the helpers after the children had been despatched home, and naturally Peter had had to follow this cosy practice, which would have been fine had it not been for Lucinda's presence, for as unworldly as he was, it had not taken him long to discover that a certain lady was making a determined bid for his attentions, and he was making just as determined a stand to avoid any such entanglement, by giving her no encouragement whatsoever.

It was not surprising therefore that Lucinda should transfer her allegiance from Diana to Rowena, and she had developed the hunter's instinct in tracking down her quarry, seeing through Peter's attachment to Rowena as the protective ploy it was, and she did not see Rowena as a rival but as a passport through the golden gate of matrimony.

By the time Rowena had worked this out, she had to admit that Lucinda had paid her the compliment of not having designs on the good-looking curate, and could be trusted as a confidante. Compliment though it was, Rowena could guess the thoughts behind it. In everyone's eyes, she was so besotted with Sean that it was unthinkable that she would turn her affections elsewhere, and she wondered what Lucinda would think if she knew the whole truth.

The situation was not a comfortable one for Rowena, and when Lucinda started throwing invitations her way, to dinner on one occasion, and tea on another, she turned both invitations down, regrettably declining on the grounds of pressure of work, for by now the village was well aware of the forthcoming hunt ball and that Rowena was doing the organising, and this gave her a perfectly good excuse.

What excuse she would find after the ball, she had no idea, but things looked decidedly tricky. She could sympathise with both parties, but came down heavily on Peter's side. Lucinda was going the wrong way about gaining his attention, at least in the way she wanted him to notice her! It would have been so much wiser, Rowena thought, if Lucinda had bided her time instead of hanging around him with her heart on her sleeve for all to see.

These thoughts inevitably brought her back to the past, and her own foolish behaviour where Sean was concerned, and she shook her head sadly; she was hardly the one to give Lucinda any advice in that direction, all she could plead was youth—she had been very young and very unsophisticated while Lucinda was of an age when she ought to know better.

It was Diana who shot the first warning arrow in Rowena's direction. Infuriated at Lucinda's desertion to the one person she had cause to dislike, she wasted no time in venting her fury on Rowena.

The attack was launched when they were alone after a basket-weaving evening at the vicarage, and Lucinda had rushed out in the hope of having a word with Peter who was seeing the children out of the vicarage. 'Haven't you done enough?' she hissed at Rowena, who stared at her in amazement at the sudden attack. 'You know what I'm talking about,' she went on furiously. 'Not content with buying your way into Sean's life, you have to ruin Lucinda's chances with Peter Roshier. Oh, I know how it is with you and Sean, and it serves you right. You didn't think he'd sink that low, did you? But I'm warning you, if you don't stay out of this and continue to encourage Peter to ignore her, then you're asking for trouble. Sean's got his pride, as you've already found out. He doesn't care one jot for you, but he does value his name. If you're up to anything, then he'll find out, and I wouldn't care to be in your shoes when he does. If you're trying to make him jealous, then you want your head examined,' she ended pithily.

After this cosy little chat, Rowena was naturally thoughtful on the way home with Peter. She knew she would have to say something about what had happened—if only to warn him what would soon be bandied around the village, because she was certain that Diana was out to make trouble for her. 'You must stop seeing me home, Peter,' she announced suddenly, making him stop in his tracks and stare at her.

'Only doing the right thing,' he replied vaguely, 'It's dark, and this hill is unlit—er—prowlers and things, you know,' he ended lamely.

'It's more the things than the prowlers, isn't it?' Rowena replied, unable to stop a note of amusement entering into her voice. 'I know the real reason, so you can stop pretending,' she added gently.

Peter started walking again when Rowena did and she felt rather than saw the shamefaced look he sent her. 'It shows, does it?' he asked pathetically.

Rowena nodded. 'I'm afraid so,' she replied, 'and although I can quite sympathise with you, you'll have to devise some other defence,' she advised him, then an idea hit her. 'Look, couldn't you drop a few hints about a girl back in your home town, Chester?' she asked brightly.

'I'm not very good at that sort of thing,' Peter replied miserably. 'I only wish there was a girl in Chester. I'm not much addicted to feminine company. In fact, women positively terrify me. Why can't they let a fellow alone?' he complained bitterly. 'When Joshua suggested I might like to take over the living of the parish, I thought it was a splendid idea. It's not so easy to find a parish these days, at least, not with a guaranteed flock to attend church. I suppose,' he added thoughtfully after a moment's silence, 'it's what every aspiring curate has to put up with until he finds the right girl to share his vocation.'

There was a companionable silence as they walked on, each busy with their thoughts, then Peter spoke again. 'It's a pity you're married,' he commented. 'I can talk to you.'

It took a second or so for what he had just said to sink in, and then he exclaimed in dismay, 'I say! Nothing's been said, has it? I mean, about my seeing you home. Has the squire said anything?'

'Good gracious, no!' Rowena assured him confidently, 'and he's not likely to. Nothing's been said,' she added, with not quite so much confidence. 'The thing is, this is a small village, and like it or not, the possibility's there, and it would be foolish to ignore it.'

'You're right, of course,' Peter commented dolefully, as they reached the drive to Tancred House. 'But do promise to come to my rescue if I look like losing out, please,' he asked Rowena earnestly, before he left her.

That was easier said than done, Rowena thought as she let herself into Tancred House, and she only hoped that she would be able to keep her promise.

CHAPTER NINE

ON the night of the hunt ball, which to Rowena's thinking had arrived with incredible speed at the end of her organising arrangements, and having satisfied herself that all was running smoothly and left the catering in the capable hands of Mrs Broom, she was now able to spend some time on her toilet and prepare herself for the evening.

Her mind was still busy on the ball, and she hoped that she had not forgotten anything important as she chose the dress that she felt most suited her, and after a quick shower she began to dress.

As she stepped into the grey velour gown that she had worn at her engagement party, she could hear the cars arriving at the front of the house, and in the background she could hear the notes of the orchestra tuning up.

Her eyes were wide and thoughtful as she gave herself a last-minute scrutiny in the mirror before going down to the hall to mingle with the guests, for she could now be an onlooker and possibly enjoy the evening. Her smooth brow creased as she thought of her father, and she devoutly hoped he would not burden Sean with his company all evening, as this would surely tax Sean's temper, which he seemed to lose rather often these days, she thought wistfully, as she recalled the few peaceful evenings that she had spent with him discussing the arrangements for the ball.

Her frown deepened as she dwelt on this puzzling aspect of his behaviour, for it was a complete turnabout to his previous decision to really get to know her, and she could only come up with the solution that he had given up his quest of discovery where she was concerned. He had obviously had to admit to defeat, and this alone, she told herself sadly, would not improve his temper, and from now on she was bound to find herself getting the raw edge of his tongue.

It was better that way, she reminded herself as she walked to the door. At least she knew where she was with him, and would not be likely to fall into any more daydreams where he was concerned.

She had only got half-way along the gallery corridor when Sean came stamping towards her. One look at his face told her that he was in a towering rage, and her mind searched for something terrible that she had forgotten to do that would put him in this mood and make him search her out like this.

The feminine side of her only saw a tall, fair, handsome man with blazing blue eyes, and, dressed in a pink hunting jacket looking perfectly splendid in spite of his rage.

'Where the devil have you been?' he demanded furiously. 'Our guests are arriving. It's the usual custom for the host and hostess to greet them,' he added caustically, then cast an eye over her dress. 'Haven't you got anything else to wear?' he demanded. 'You wore that dress at our engagement party,' he added accusingly.

Rowena was still recovering from his earlier remarks and how he had expected her to welcome his guests. They were his guests, not hers, she thought. She stared down at her dress—what had he said about it? He hadn't liked it, that was certain. 'Shall I change it?' she asked vaguely, quite expecting him to go off the deep end again and say something sarcastic about keeping the guests waiting at her convenience.

Sean gave a curt nod. 'And make it something brighter,' he ordered autocratically. 'You could have asked me for a dress,' he added harshly, 'and it wouldn't have come out of Southall funds either!' With that he strode off with a brusque command that she be 'quick about it.'

Rowena went back to her rooms in a daze. She wished she knew why Sean was insisting on her sharing the honours with him, and she also wished she knew a little more about the etiquette on such occasions. As far as she knew, as long as the hostess was around somewhere making the guests comfortable and seeing to their needs, a duty that she had intended to carry out anyway, she could see no point in standing by the door individually welcoming the guests like royalty.

She gave a deep sigh as she searched in her wardrobe for a suitable dress. She did not see much chance of a happy evening now that she had broken the first code of etiquette, and goodness knew how many others during the course of the evening.

Her search revealed a sea-blue velvet dress that she had only worn once but had felt was too startling a blue for her, and drew it out of the wardrobe. 'Something brighter', Sean had said, and this was certainly bright.

After she had slipped into the dress, she placed a double row of pearls around her neck, an inheritance from her mother, then stood back to look at the result. Her wide eyes held a hint of surprise in them as she surveyed the grand-looking woman staring back at her in the mirror. 'Not at all like me,' she muttered, as she gave her hair a final brush and left the bedroom, half expecting to find Sean waiting outside, but he was nowhere in sight as she hurried down to the hall.

By the time she reached the hall the guests had moved on to the ballroom, and Rowena quickened her steps, for Sean was sure to be further irritated at her for taking so long to change.

The orchestra had started playing the first dance as she reached the ballroom, and she drew in a breath of wonder at the sight that met her eyes as she advanced into the huge oak-panelled room, the chandeliers of which reflected the jewels worn by the women, and their no less splendid dresses.

The pink coats of the hunting fraternity were very prominent among the swirling guests on the dance floor, and Rowena could see Sean at the far corner of the room surrounded by a sea of red coats.

She hadn't know that Sean was a member of the hunt, she thought sadly; she really didn't know much about him at all. In all probability he was the hunt master, and although she did not care much for their activities, she had to admit that the regalia was most becoming.

There were so many people in the ballroom that it was doubtful that anyone noticed Rowena standing by the door uncertain whether to make her way to Sean or just mingle with the guests. When her eye caught Mrs Marsden, seated in an alcove a little way along the room, she cowardly chose to mingle, and made her way towards the vicar's wife, seeing the vicar standing a little way away from her and in earnest conversation with a man Rowena had met but whose name she had forgotten. Peter was nowhere to be seen, and Rowena wondered if Lucinda had finally caught up with him, and if so, what she could do about it, in view of her promise to him.

Happily for Peter no such fate had befallen him, and he was taking good care that it wouldn't, for only a minute or so after Rowena had joined Mrs Marsden he appeared from nowhere and joined in the discussion. Rowena had a suspicion that he had found himself a bolthole to which he could retreat whenever danger threatened.

'Rowena, you look exceptionally pretty this evening,' exclaimed Mrs Marsden, 'and that dress is very becoming on you. I do so love a splash of colour,' she exclaimed as she looked round at the crowded assembly. 'Isn't it all so splendid!' she remarked, 'takes me back to my youth. There were lots of hunt balls in those days, you know,' and she gave a little sigh, 'it's different now, of course,' and gave Rowena a sweet smile, 'but things are looking up. Have you seen Diana and Lucinda?' she asked Rowena, and Rowena saw Peter cast a hurried glance around them ready to leave at the given signal. 'Diana's got a beautiful dress on. White and gold, and I shouldn't be surprised if Lucinda hadn't had a hand in helping her make it. I think perhaps that Lucinda's dress is a shade too dark a red for her, but as long as she feels it suits her that's all that matters,' she added kindly.

Peter had moved away at the start of this conversation and stationed himself beside the vicar, but when Rowena moved on from Mrs Marsden, he rejoined her. 'It's all a bit much, isn't it?' he commented with a grin. 'Such grandeur, with all the austerity there is in the country at the present time. Do they really hold these sort of do's often?' he queried.

'As Mrs Marsden said,' replied Rowena, 'in the days gone by, as often as they could. Hunt balls, I gather, only once a year, but even that had to be dropped when the coffers ran out.' She followed Peter's eyes as he stared around the assembly. 'I would say your bells are as good as ordered,' she said smilingly. 'Sean said a lot of people had sent contributions as well as coming to the ball.'

'In that case,' Peter replied with a smile, 'I hope they all enjoy themselves.' He was still smiling as he gave another look about him, then he drew in a quick breath. 'Oh, lor'!' he groaned despondently, and the next moment he had led Rowena on to the dance floor, asking a little belatedly if she would care to dance, adding apologetically that he could only dance a waltz, and he rather thought that that was what they were playing.

In point of fact it was a quickstep, but as Rowena was not much of a dancer herself, it didn't make much difference. One look back as they took to the dance floor explained the reason for Peter's hurried exit the only way left open to him, for Mrs Dean and Lucinda were looking their way and had obviously just arrived.

It was not so much dancing as trying to avoid tripping over Peter's feet that seemed to be everywhere but where they should be, and Rowena was torn between an urge to giggle at the farcical situation she had landed in, and an urgent wish to make Peter face up to his responsibilities, if that was what Lucinda could be called. He just couldn't go on with the disappearing act if he intended to take over on the vicar's retirement. 'For goodness' sake, Peter!' she got out breathlessly, having just missed a collision with another couple on the floor; it was not easy trying to see where Peter's feet were, and watch out for collisions. 'You can't go on like this, it's ridiculous!' she scolded him.

'I don't get much opportunity to learn dancing,' Peter replied, wilfully misunderstanding Rowena's meaning.

'You know what I'm talking about,' Rowena replied, wincing as he trod on her foot. 'You can be polite without committing yourself to matrimony, can't you?' she asked exasperatedly.

'There are ways,' he muttered darkly, fixing his gaze on the back of a member of the hunt who had just jostled him, then stared back at where Lucinda and her mother still stood waiting for them to come off the floor at the end of the dance, and looked away hastily as Lucinda waved at him. 'That is her mother with her, isn't it?' he queried gloomily, as he steadied Rowena and waited until she had got her step back again. 'I suppose,' he asked indifferently, 'you couldn't put it around that I come from a very eccentric family, or something on those lines? Not on dear old Joshua's side,' he added quickly, 'I wouldn't want to give that impression.'

Rowena swallowed, but this time she couldn't stop a chuckle bursting out. 'Even slightly dotty?' she got out, knowing she was encouraging him, but unable to do anything about it. All it needed now, she told herself, was for her to fall flat on her face as she had very nearly done a moment or so ago when Peter had saved her, and thinking of Sean's fury at the spectacle her amusement increased instead of abating. What had she said about the Southalls giving value for money? she thought almost hysterically, although she hadn't planned to be part of the entertainment. 'Oh, Peter, you're priceless!' she managed to get out as the dance ended, and in an effort to bring some kind of sanity into a situation that looked like getting out of hand, she glanced back at where Lucinda and her mother had been standing. They were still there, but so was Sean, and her eyes, that had been alight with laughter a second or so ago, now immediately sobered as they met Sean's narrowed gaze.

For one moment Rowena contemplated follow-

ing Peter's urgent wish that they should go in the
opposite direction from where the reception committee awaited them, but she managed to pull herself together and led the way towards them, saying
in a soothing voice to Peter that she doubted that
Lucinda would expect him to repeat his perform-
ance on the dance floor, not if she had any regard
for him, that was, and in a much lower voice advised him to circulate as soon as he could get
away.

After a few polite words with Peter, Sean
dragged Rowena away—at least that was how it
felt to her as he escorted her from group to group,
introducing her to people she would never remember the names of, and hardly ever see, since
most of the strangers came from neighbouring vil-
lages and were mostly members of the hunt.

When they had reached the end of the room,
Rowena saw that her father was in the next group
Sean intended to introduce her to, expounding on
the art of horsemanship, and how he hadn't ridden
for years but might well take it up again, his eyes
on the splendid pink coat of the man next to him.
Oh dear, Rowena thought with a pang of anxiety,
he was thinking of joining the hunt, she was sure
of it, and really he ought to be taking things
easy, not charging about the countryside on a
horse.

She felt rather than saw Sean's irritation on
finding her father holding forth in the group, and
with skilful ease he steered her away from the
group and on to the dance floor.

The movement was so reminiscent of Peter's
action a short while ago that Rowena was back to

the giggling stage, and wondered why her sense of humour should let her down at this time; she was not normally like this.

'Something amusing you?' Sean queried with raised brows as he took her into his arms for the start of the dance.

As his arms went round Rowena she lost all trace of amusement as a wave of panic went through her, and she wondered if this was his first dance of the evening or if he had danced with Diana, who had, as Mrs Marsden had said, looked perfectly lovely in her white and gold creation. She thought of anything but the strong hold of Sean's hand as it held her small one, and the feel of his other arm around her waist. 'It was something Peter said,' she replied, not realising how stiff her words sounded, not natural at all. 'It just struck me as funny,' she added lamely.

'So I noticed,' Sean said softly, as he swung her into the tempo of the dance. 'You certainly couldn't have been enjoying the dance. I wondered how he dared take the floor.'

'There was a good reason,' Rowena got out before she realised it, then had to swallow hard, because a giggle had almost slipped out; this time it was hysteria, she thought wildly, and hoped that Sean would say something disparaging that would sober her.

She got her wish, but not in the way she had hoped. Sean's arm around her waist tightened and he drew her close to him. Her first reaction was one of shock, and her brown eyes widened as she stared up at him, plainly asking for an explanation for such behaviour since she could not very well push him away, not under the full gaze of the whole room.

'Dear old Dad's watching,' he said silkily. 'The Tancreds give value for money too,' he added softly, as his hand tightened on hers. 'I like that dress,' he went on smoothly, 'it was just what I had in mind. You'll do fine as long as you do what you're told—and that reminds me,' he added, ignoring Rowena's gasp of indignation at the way he had made her feel part of a circus act, and had just learnt a new trick, 'there's something I want to have a word with you on later.'

That was all he said, and Rowena, still smarting from his backhanded compliment, surmised that it was something to do with the ball, something else she had slipped up on, but she was past caring; the evening had turned into a synthetic adventure for her. Like her marriage it was not real, and she longed for her freedom.

Her father hardly helped to revive her spirits by telling her that he had heard from David, and that he was expecting him the following weekend.

It was all Rowena needed to make her evening, but she could not have foreseen that there was worse to come, or she would have headed for her rooms then and there, protocol or no protocol!

When the ball eventually came to an end during the early hours of the morning, Rowena stood next to Sean as they saw the guests off the premises. He had made certain that she would be present for this last duty to their guests by keeping her close to his side for the last waltz and the culmination of the evening.

Had she been in a happier frame of mind she

would have been able to appreciate the many compliments expressed by the guests for a splendid evening, but as it was, the words flowed over her head and meant nothing to her, since it was Sean they were really thanking, not her.

Her father's goodnight and 'don't forget about David,' added to her misery. As if she could forget, she thought wearily, for she was no nearer a solution to her problem in that direction, and so much had happened since he had written that she had hardly had time to work out a plausible excuse for her extraordinary living arrangements.

After the orchestra had also departed and Mrs Broom and an army of helpers had begun to attack the remnants from the catering efforts, doing the odd jobs that couldn't be left until the next day, Sean turned his attention to Rowena, who could have fallen asleep on her feet. 'Come into the drawing-room,' he ordered, and at her look of exasperation, not to mention tiredness, he added, 'it won't take long, and certainly won't wait until some later date, probably in a week's time, whenever I happen to catch sight of you either going out or coming in. You've been rather a busy little bee lately, haven't you?' he said silkily.

Mostly on his account, Rowena thought silently as she followed his stiff erect back out of the ballroom. She had had to do a lot of chasing about, visiting the caterers, getting the invitations printed, and a hundred other little jobs that had needed constant monitoring, but by the way he had said that, it had sounded as if she had gone out of her way to keep out of his vicinity, which was hardly fair, and even it was true, surely it had been

what he had wanted. She sighed inwardly.
Something was wrong, and Sean was taking it out
on her. Whatever it was, she hoped he would get
it over with, for she was desperately tired.

When she did not answer he went on, 'It's come
to my notice that you've been seeing a lot of Peter
Roshier these last few weeks.'

Rowena was now fully awake and she stared
back at Sean. Diana, she thought, had not wasted
any time in carrying out her threat. Peter singling
her out for his one and only dance must have so
infuriated her that she had deliberately set out to
make trouble for her, not that she would succeed
where Rowena was concerned, but Peter was a different matter.

'Idle gossip,' she retorted furiously. 'I'm surprised you took any notice of it,' she shrugged her
slim shoulders. 'Someone noticed that Peter paid
me the courtesy of seeing me home from the evening classes at the vicarage—and that's all there is
to it!' she ended scathingly.

'The "someone" happens to be me,' Sean said
softly, and at Rowena's startled glance back at
him, he nodded grimly. 'And you're right, people
know me a little too well to indulge in the pastime
of idle gossip.'

Rowena felt a spurt of alarm on Peter's behalf.
If he wanted the living of the parish he hadn't exactly made a good start by alienating the squire. 'I
do assure you that there's nothing——' she began
hastily, but Sean interrupted her.

'Give me some credit for intelligence,' he bit
back harshly. 'I'm fully aware of that. What's
worrying me is your reaction to his attention.

You're rather partial to fair men, aren't you?' he taunted. 'I just wanted to make sure that you were aware of the situation, and that he's using you as a cover.'

Rowena blinked, then swallowed. Of all the detestable men—and to think of the times in her room when she had almost gone soft on him! Here he was, telling her in no uncertain fashion that he was under no illusion that Peter had formed a romantic attachment to her, her attractions didn't rate that high! He just didn't want her to make a fool of herself was what it really amounted to—as if he cared! she thought furiously. 'Of course I know he's using me!' she got out, almost stammering in her fury. 'The poor man's being hounded by Lucinda Dean—but I suppose you know that too,' she ended bitterly.

Sean nodded complacently. 'As a fellow sufferer I do know what that feels like, and I have some sympathy for him. I don't want you to get involved, he'll have to work out his own salvation. I think perhaps Diana will be able to help out here,' he added musingly. 'She's more cut out for that kind of role, not that I can see her becoming a vicar's wife, and she'll probably be the next person we shall have to rescue, but I think she'll be able to handle things—she's certainly had a lot of practice casting off unwanted suitors,' he added comfortably.

Rowena wanted to scream at him that because he found Diana attractive and was probably in love with her, he was of the opinion that no man could resist her. In the end she spoke quite calmly and rather surprised herself. 'I don't think that will work. Oh, I agree with you about Diana's attractions, but in this case it simply won't do. Peter only wants to be left alone to get on with his job. I'm sure Lucinda will eventually realise that only time will help her cause,' she added, with as much dignity as she could muster.

'I very much doubt that,' Sean replied sarcastically, obviously annoyed with Rowena for refusing to consider his plan. 'I'm inclined to think that she feels that if she's persistent enough she'll get what she wants.'

Rowena's brown eyes met Sean's mocking ones. She was fully aware of what he had been referring to—her marriage to him. 'As in my case?' she asked quietly.

Sean gave a nonchalant shrug of his powerful shoulders. 'It's possible that her thinking is running on those lines,' he admitted callously.

'If I thought that was the case,' Rowena replied steadily, in spite of the fact that her unhappiness threatened to overwhelm her, 'I would have a greater sympathy with Lucinda than with Peter, and I'd most certainly do my utmost to prevent her from making a disastrous mistake. I would advise her,' she went on recklessly, wanting to hurt him as much as he had hurt her, 'to take a good look at me. I can't think of any better way to bring her to her senses, can you?' she asked, bringing a bittersweet note into her voice, and did not wait for his reply, which came in the form of punitive action. She managed to avoid his sudden move towards her, and with wings on her feet flew off to her rooms, not stopping to take breath until she had bolted the door behind her.

When her heart had stopped thudding, reaction set in and tears cascaded down her cheeks, and after she had had her cry and felt a little better, she tried to get down to some serious thinking.

It was obvious that things couldn't go on like this, but she couldn't see what could be done about it. It would be no use appealing to her father to get her out of what was becoming an impossible situation for her, not after Sean's deliberate show of affection on the dance floor in front of him, although why he had bothered to do that was beyond her comprehension unless— Rowena's tear-drenched eyes opened a fraction wider as she suddenly got the answer. Diana! It had to be that!

There had hardly been a dance that she had missed. She recalled seeing her partnered by most of the younger members of the hunt, by Sean too, for she had thought how well they had danced together, but as far as she knew Sean had only had one dance with her; under the circumstances he had had to be content with that. How galling it must have been for him to watch Diana receiving the admiration and attendance from the younger bloods while he was powerless to send them about their business, having now lost that right.

She nodded her head sadly. It had been his way of getting back at Diana when he had held Rowena close to him. He hadn't cared one whit about her father. He was not a man to curry that sort of favour, not even to a man he was in debt to.

His suggestion that Diana would be the person to help out in Peter's dilemma only went to show

how sure he was of her. He had not even entertained the notion that Diana might fall in love with Peter—how could she when she was in love with him?

Rowena drew in a ragged breath. On this point she was in entire agreement with him. Peter was too sensitive a man to attract a woman like Diana, who would want to be completely dominated by her man.

Rowena twisted the handkerchief that she held in her hand and had now reduced to a damp rag. She had to talk to someone about her troubles, and who better than her brother David. He would bring some kind of sense into the situation she had landed herself in, and it wasn't too late to extricate her from it.

Sean was as unhappy as she was, she was certain of it, although he was not likely to reveal his inner thoughts to such as her, only make her the butt for his frustrated feelings, and that was why he had brought the subject of Peter up, not because he was worried over their association, but because he wanted a whipping boy to vent his fury on.

CHAPTER TEN

DURING the next few days Rowena made a point of avoiding Sean, even to the extent of not going to collect Goldie for her walk in the mornings, a habit she had still retained even though, as Sean had said, there was no need as Goldie always accompanied him on his early morning rides.

On the third day, however, she found Goldie in the hall when she got downstairs, and she wondered who had let her in the front of the house. As Sean sauntered through from the main section of the house, Rowena had the answer.

'Goldie and I have missed you,' he said grandly, his blue eyes meeting hers in what appeared to be an accusing way. 'So we thought,' he went on gravely, 'that we ought to find out if everything was all right.'

Rowena continued to look at him and in the end was forced to drop her gaze and bend down to give Goldie a hug. 'Well, as you see, I'm fine,' she said quickly, and added hurriedly, 'I was on my way to pay a call on Miss Heysham. I seem to have neglected her lately. She'll want to hear all about the ball, her arthritis was playing up and she had to miss it,' she babbled on, refusing to be intimidated by a certain look in Sean's eyes.

'I've half a mind to come with you,' Sean declared smoothly, raising his brows at the look of astonishment on Rowena's face quickly followed by another look that plainly said 'Oh, no!' 'However,' he continued, this time with a glint in his eyes, 'I'm afraid pressure of work prevents such an outing. Do give her my regards, won't you? Er—Goldie's lead is on the table,' he added offhandedly.

Rowena gave a stiff nod and went to collect it, wishing Sean would take himself off to all that work he had mentioned, but he stood where he was until she left the house and she felt in some odd indefinable way that she had just walked out on him and that she ought not to have done.

She gave a deep sigh as she walked down the

drive. What an exceedingly difficult man he was, she thought. Tormenting her one minute, and the next, making it appear that it was all her fault.

By the time she had reached the end of the drive and started to walk down the hill towards the village, she had pushed Sean and his unpredictable ways out of her mind and had gone back to the subject that had filled her thoughts since the night of the ball—David's visit.

No matter how the reason for the marriage was explained, it was going to come as a shock to him, and after she had rehearsed several times in her mind how she could put it to him, it had sounded worse with each rendering. No amount of glossing over the facts would hide the bald unpalatable truth that it was a marriage of convenience where Sean was concerned, and a ghastly mistake on hers. At least that was how David would see it and even that was preferable to the truth, but how could she expect David to help her if he didn't know the truth?

Rowena had no answer to that, any more than she had the answer for anything else that concerned her marriage. She ought to have gone to David when her father had first thrown the arrangement at her. Now it was too late, and it was hardly fair to expect him to work the oracle.

So that was that. Rowena took in a deep breath. She had known what she was going to do all along the way, even while working out what she was going to tell David, and now that she had come to terms with it in her own mind, she almost felt relieved.

There was no reason why David should suspect

it was anything else but a normal marriage. She could be sure of Sean's absence, he never visited her in her rooms, and David was not familiar with Tancred House, so he could not possibly know that Rowena was living in another part of the house.

Her mind raced on. She would order tea for two, and had to hope that he called in the afternoon, rather than the evening—in fact, she would make a point of asking her father to tell him to call in the afternoon. An evening call would be very tricky where Sean was concerned, and she almost stopped in her tracks at the thought that David might expect to be asked to dinner, but she doubted this. He hated social occasions and would be rather relieved, she suspected, by the non-appearance of the man she had married, for he hated small talk too, and would accept Rowena's apologies on behalf of Sean's absence—on some pretext or other, say an urgent call from one of his farms—with grateful relief.

It had to work, she thought desperately; there was no other way. Fate had not been very kind to her lately and surely it was time that her luck changed.

Although she did call on Miss Heysham, her mind was far away from the conversation and it was very difficult not to wander off the subject and lapse into silence at the wrong time. Only Miss Heysham's anxious enquiry if everything was all right jerked her back to the present and made her make an effort to apply her attention to the conversation.

When Friday dawned Rowena was in an agony

of nerves, because this was the day David would
be arriving home, and would be calling in on her
during the afternoon. Certain that all that could
go wrong, would go wrong, she was torn between
waiting for him to arrive or going to meet him
before he reached the house, but quickly abandoned the idea of going to meet him in the
grounds, as the chances were that she would run
into Sean whom she had successfully avoided since
his appearance in the hall two days ago.

To avoid giving the impression of isolation,
Rowena had arranged to collect the tea tray from
the kitchen instead of having it sent up by the
dining-room hatch, for she did not want David to
see that part of the arrangement, for once he had
seen the small dining area the game would be up,
and all Rowena's plans would come to nothing.

David was fifteen minutes late, and Rowena,
hovering in the hall ready to sweep him up to her
quarters, began to form a horrible suspicion that
he had been waylaid by Sean and to wonder what
she was going to do about it if he had.

The swish of tires on the gravelled drive outside
the house immediately quashed this unwelcome
thought, and not waiting for him to ring the bell,
she had opened the door before he had got out of
the car and stood waiting for him.

'My, my,' said David, after giving Rowena a
quick bear-hug. 'We've come up in the world,
haven't we? Tea and crumpets now, I presume?' he
teased her affectionately, as he allowed himself to
be led up the grand staircase to her rooms.

Rowena asked him about the art college, and
how he was getting on, and why hadn't he written

more often, and would he please do something about his writing, it was hardly legible, etc.—in fact, anything but the one subject she dreaded, that of her marriage.

When David attempted to stop and look at the paintings in the gallery, she kept on walking, hoping that he would not ask any questions about the illustrious-looking past members of the Tancred family, for she would be unable to identify them, and to her relief he followed her into her apartment with an amused comment of her having a lot to live up to.

Once they were in her rooms Rowena gave a little sigh of relief. The first part of the scheme had succeeded, and as she saw David cast a look about him, taking note of the Hepplewhite sofa, she was almost certain of success, but she did wish the lounge looked a little more lived in.

'Are you happy?' demanded David, making her glance quickly away from his searching deep blue eyes before she answered.

'Of course,' she replied, giving him a bright smile. 'So much has happened, I hardly know where to begin.' That part was true anyway, she thought miserably. 'I'm sorry Sean's not around,' she went on quickly. 'There was an emergency on one of the farms,' she added, as she saw David give her an assessing look. That was the trouble with trying to fool someone who knew you, she thought wretchedly. 'How long are you staying?' she asked.

'I'm off tomorrow,' he answered. 'Dad made a lame effort to get me to stay longer, but happily the arrangements are made and I could refuse.' He gave a wide grin. 'I gather he's thinking of joining the local hunt. Muttered something about seeing a man about a horse.'

Rowena shook her head slowly. 'It's the hunt ball that started that,' she explained. 'I believe he took a fancy to the pink jackets,' she added with a twinkle in her eye, then looked serious again. 'I do hope he doesn't overdo it. His doctor did advise him to take it easy.'

'Oh, I shouldn't worry on that score,' David advised her comfortably. 'He's as tough as old boots, and certainly not stupid enough to risk all for the sake of a pink coat. What's the betting he lands himself a nice easy billet in the hunt on the organising side?' he added with a grin.

'That would be more like it,' Rowena agreed with a smile, and suddenly remembered the tea. 'I won't be a moment,' she said quickly as she went to the door, adding lightly just before she left him, 'I do hope Mrs Broom thought of crumpets!'

When she had closed the door behind her, she fairly raced down the gallery and down the stairs to the kitchen to collect the tea tray, hoping Mrs Broom would have it ready for her. But being Mrs Broom, she had not let her down; all that was needed was to pour the water into the silver teapot, and this she did as soon as she saw Rowena, and everything was ready.

In spite of the weight of the tray Rowena made good time on her return journey, but she almost dropped it when she caught sight of the tall form of Sean a little way ahead of her when she reached the gallery. 'Sean!' she exclaimed, keeping her voice as low as she dared, and when he turned and waited for her to reach him, she gave a deep sigh of relief. Whatever he had to say to her could be said outside in the gallery without fear of him meeting David, and just wasn't it like him to decide to call on her at that time, she thought exasperatedly—he had never done so before.

When she reached him, he took the tray from her before she had time to realise his intention, and although it had been heavy she was annoyed at his action. 'What do you want?' she asked him, still in a low voice. 'I've got a visitor at the moment. Couldn't it wait until later?' she demanded.

Sean's blue eyes narrowed, showing his displeasure at her obvious wish to get rid of him. 'I saw a car,' he replied smoothly. 'I rather thought it might be David.'

'It is!' Rowena almost hissed at him, attempting to take the tray away from Sean.

'Then why on earth didn't you bring him to the main quarters?' Sean demanded haughtily, refusing to part with the tray.

'And ask your permission to entertain my own brother? No, thank you!' she returned acidly. 'I told him you'd been called away, so you don't have to put in an appearance,' she added, with a trace of pleading in her voice that Sean chose to ignore.

'No trouble, in fact I'm looking forward to meeting him again. He is my brother-in-law isn't he?' he commented casually, and looked down at the tray he was holding. 'You'd better call down to Mrs Broom and ask her to add another cup to this

lot—she can send it up in the hatch,' he added loftily.

Rowena closed her eyes. As long as Sean kept
away she knew she would be able to keep up the
charade, but with him there—— 'Please,' she said
quietly, and this time there was no mistaking the
urgency behind the plea. 'Please leave us alone. It
will look so odd if you turn up now.'

Sean's blond brows rose. 'Are you sure it is your
brother in there, and not Peter Roshier?' he demanded, and before Rowena could stop him he
had marched to the door of her rooms and opened
it.

With lagging steps, Rowena was forced to
follow him, and as she heard David say, 'So the
wanderer returns,' to Sean as he held his hand out
towards him. 'Everything all right in the farm
line?' he queried, as he shook hands with him, and
she had to put on a bright smile, although she felt
more like weeping.

It was like walking a tightrope and knowing
that you were going to fall off, she thought despondently as she listened to Sean asking David
how he enjoyed college, and started to pour out
the tea, only remembering that she hadn't enough
cups to go round, and having to make a quick
dash into the dining room and call down to Mrs
Brown to send up another cup for Mr Sean.

There was no chance of David overhearing the
request, for she had carefully closed the door of
the lounge behind her, and when Mrs Broom com-
plied with the request, she slipped back into the
lounge, noticing with grateful relief that the men
were still on the subject of art, Sean mentioning a
few fine paintings that he had managed to hang on

to in spite of the state of the economy.

Having completed her duties and handed round the tea, Rowena sat back and listened to the conversation, lulled into a soothing realisation that all would be well, and it was quite possible that Sean would invite David to dinner, and if he did, it would be served in Sean's dining room, which would certainly be more in keeping with what her position called for, and she would have no worries of David finding out the truth.

All might have been well, had it not been for Mrs Broom, who, with her usual thoroughness, intended to make sure that the master of the house did not go without his tea, and took it upon herself to carry a second tray up to Rowena's room, and when admitted, and carrying in the tray, she remarked cheerfully to Sean, 'I left yours in the drawing-room. I couldn't think where you'd got to until Mrs Tancred told me you were in her apartment.'

Rowena remembered giving a stiff-sounding, 'Thank you, Mrs Broom,' before she left them, not realising that she had just blown Rowena's cover sky-high. Rowena also remembered looking at Sean and thinking vaguely that he hadn't moved a muscle, and then she looked at David who was staring at her.

'So I was right,' he said quietly, as he looked from Sean to Rowena. 'I had a brief look round while you were getting the tea,' he told Rowena, 'and this is the nearest thing to a granny flat that I've seen.' He transferred his gaze to Sean. 'Are you married?' he asked, still with that deadly quietness that Rowena recognised from old, and heralded a first-class row, all in fact that she had dreaded.

'I think it would be a good idea if we had a talk in private,' said Sean, matching David's tone. 'The situation is rather a complicated one.'

'Who for?' David queried, and this time there was no mistaking the animosity in his voice or in his glance as he looked at Sean. 'For you, or my sister?'

'David, please,' Rowena broke in. 'I'm sure Sean can explain everything, and if he can't, then ask Father,' she added, unable to prevent the bitterness entering her voice.

'What the devil has Dad to do with this?' David queried, then his eyes opened a shade wider and he clapped a hand to his head. 'Am I slow?' he said, and looked back at Rowena. 'I can see why the old man wanted to break into society, but what happened to you? And don't tell me you were still nursing a crush on Tancred. I know you too well for that,' he warned her.

Rowena swallowed. This was worse than she had imagined. She sent Sean a pleading look. 'I'd like to talk to my brother alone, please,' she requested.

Sean's face hardened and she knew he was going to refuse to leave them. 'I think I have the right to be present,' he said haughtily.

'As these are my sister's rooms, I think not,' David retorted hotly.

'In my house,' Sean replied softly, his rapier glance clashing with David's furious one.

'Yours with the help of my father's money, if I read the whole mess right!' David flung back at him. 'I've got the measure of it now. It's the only thing that makes sense, from your point of view, but——' he sent Rowena a helpless look. 'You might as well tell me the whole of it,' he said firmly. 'I'm not leaving until you do.'

'Please David, not now,' Rowena pleaded.

'Now!' repeated David. 'How the devil can I help you if I don't know the score? You no more belong here than I do, or Dad if it comes to that—not that that would worry him, not when he gets a bee in his bonnet.'

Rowena licked her dry lips and gave a helpless shrug. 'Well, you know Father,' she began in a low voice, and her eyes went to Sean now sitting comfortably in one of the fireside chairs, and the thought struck her that he was as interested in hearing her explanation as David was. He did not look a bit embarrassed, and surely he ought to have been, she thought bewilderedly. 'Well, he'd remembered——' She swallowed; it was what she had wanted, wasn't it? She had wanted to talk to someone about the whole wretched affair in the hope that she could receive help, but she hadn't bargained for Sean's presence. '—He'd remembered that there once was a time when I thought a lot of Sean,' she hesitated again, hating Sean for making her go through this with him present, and drew in a deep breath, wanting to get it over with in the shortest possible time. 'He rather thought it might be a good idea if we married, and just went ahead with the arrangements, after talking to Sean about it, of course,' she ended lamely, and stared miserably at the floor.

'I've got that part of it,' David said impatiently, and gave Sean a scathing look. 'What I want to know is why you let yourself be talked into it. And don't just tell me you thought it was a good idea too—that won't wear, not with me,' he threatened.

Rowena closed her eyes. This was the worst part and somehow she had to get through it. She wasn't sure, but she was almost certain that Sean had leaned forward in his chair in what seemed an expectant attitude. 'It's not going to help, David,' she said pleadingly. 'Couldn't we just leave it at that?' But at David's slow but firm shake of the head, she had to go through with it. 'Very well then, when I turned the whole idea down, he started muttering obscure references to you, and saying how he thought it was time you stopped playing around at art college and came into the family business,' she gave the appalled David a helpless look. 'I told him it was too late to do that, you'd passed your exams for the Slade and there was nothing he could do about that.' She swallowed. 'He agreed on that, but said you'd find it hard going without funds.' Her hands twisted together. 'I could see he meant it. I could also see what it would be like for you. You'd have to leave that lovely studio, and look for lodgings, and probably have to work in the evenings washing-up in some dingy café until the early hours of the morning——'

'There ought to be a violin playing somewhere in the background,' David interrupted her exasperatedly. 'My poor idiot! You didn't really think he'd cut me off without a shilling, did you? And if he did, what the devil do you think I'd care? I'd get by, thousands of others have to, and I'd a damn sight rather that than have you incarcerated in this great tomb of past Tancreds.' He glared at Sean. 'I make no apology,' he said fiercely. 'The only thing I thank you for is being enough of a gentleman to preserve my sister's rights, but I think the farce has gone on long enough, don't you think?' he demanded of Sean, and strode to the door. 'I think a good long talk with my father is called for,' he said grimly, 'and the sooner the better.' He looked at Rowena. 'Don't worry, Sis, I'll have you out of this mess before the day's out,' he assured her.

'It's not as easy as that,' Rowena called to him as he reached the door. 'There were strings attached,' she added desperately, 'it wasn't all to do with you,' casting Sean a look of pleading, and hoping for his interception before David took his father to task. He ought to know the conditions laid down at the time of the marriage, and Sean was the person to point this out, but to her indignation he remained silent, as if he was just an interested onlooker and had no part in the business at all, and it was so unlike him that Rowena was forced to come to the miserable conclusion that he was of the same opinion as David, that enough was enough, and if David could release both of them from their misery, then he would heartily congratulate him.

'I'm way ahead of you,' David replied steadily. 'I know my father, perhaps a little better than you do,' he told Rowena. 'His head's firmly stuck in the sand right now, but I intend to make him take it out and take a good look around him. He's not going to like what he sees, but it's time he heard a few home truths! Be seeing you,' and with that he quietly closed the door behind him.

Rowena was torn between an urge to run after David and try and warn him of the consequences that would follow the break-up of the contract, and a burning desire to slate Sean for his unco-operative attitude, and in the end she settled for Sean, as David was hardly likely to listen to her now that he had got the bit between his teeth. 'Thank you for your help,' she said bitterly. 'I don't know what I would have done without it!'

Sean did not answer this sarcastic rebuke but just looked at her. 'So that was the hold your father had on you, was it?' he said quietly. 'I've wanted to know that for some time, and you could have told me.'

Rowena stared at him. 'Would it have made any difference?' she queried bitterly. 'I don't think you would have believed me if I had told you. You were too certain that I'd engineered the whole thing.'

'Under the circumstances,' he replied quietly, 'I could hardly do anything else, but it's one thing to find yourself saddled with a bride that you suspect of having an ulterior motive for the marriage, and quite another to learn that you were blackmailed into it!' he ended harshly.

Rowena caught the bitterness behind his words and felt immediately contrite. It must have looked that way to him, she thought, going back to the beginning of their relationship, thanks to her father's pushing ways. 'I could have contacted David,' she said quickly, 'as he said. I was an idiot. In all probability Father wouldn't have carried out his threat,' she ended lamely, entirely forgetting that there had been more pressing reasons why she had to go through with the marriage, and not the least of these had been Sean's cold ultimatum of ruining her father if she backed out.

'Of course he wouldn't!' Sean replied ironically, 'No more than he gave me any other option but to marry his daughter!' His eyes travelled over Rowena's flushed features. 'But it was not quite so straightforward as that, was it?' he reminded her. 'I seem to recall doing a little pressuring myself,' he said softly, 'and for that I apologise. Had I known the full sum of it, no doubt some solution would have been found.' He was silent for a moment or so, then he said abruptly, 'I like David. He's a man after my own heart, and I applaud the way he came to his sister's rescue, I couldn't have done better myself,' he added musingly.

Rowena looked away quickly; her mind was on the deadlock between Sean and her father. One of them had to drop the conditions stated in the contract to bring about the solution he had mentioned, and if David was successful in making her father withdraw his previous proviso of marriage to his daughter as a condition for his financial assistance, then it was up to Sean to follow suit, and of course he would, she thought, and wondered why the thought depressed her. She was on the brink of obtaining her freedom, for she was certain that David would not fail her. She could go back to being ordinary Rowena Southall again, leading a quiet uneventful life and not having to avoid the handsome squire on his rounds round the property, but she would avoid him, she thought miserably, unable to bear the thought of suddenly meeting him in the village street when they would be awfully polite to each other, and on Sean's part go thankfully on his way after the preliminary meeting. 'It's like waiting for the countdown,' she said breathlessly, unaware that Sean had been closely observing her.

'Don't look so worried,' he said lightly. 'I'm rather looking forward to the blast-off,' he added, as he walked to the door, leaving her staring into space as he closed it behind him.

That was all it meant to him, Rowena thought dully. Right now he was probably on his way to the wine cellar to look for a bottle of the best vintage ready for the celebration, and she wondered if he would get Diana to share it with him! In her mind's eyes she could see the two of them holding up their glasses in salutation to each other and their happy future.

'Hurry up, David!' she whispered urgently, and stared at the telephone, for she was expecting an angry call from her father, demanding to know just what she had been telling David, and she had better get over there right away and make some sort of sense of it all.

By the time she had waited almost an hour for the call to come through, she was certain that David had failed to get his father to listen to reason, and when she heard a knock on her door she went to open it with listless steps, expecting to see David standing there with a look of utter frustration on his face, and as she opened the door to admit, as she thought, her brother, she wondered what other suggestion David might have to the solution, but it was not David who stood there, but her father, with what Rowena could only describe as a sheepish expression on his face.

It was so unlike him that she felt almost sorry
for him. David had been as good as his word, it
appeared, and had obviously shaken him. 'Well,
girl,' he began uncertainly, before he looked about
him and then back at Rowena. 'Seems I've been a
bit of an old fool,' he went on, then he added tet-
chily, 'Tancred's not the man I thought he was,
either. Could have changed things, but from what
I hear he couldn't care less. Dammit, he married
you, didn't he?' he demanded irritably.

'Only because he had to,' Rowena reminded him
steadily. 'It was a business arrangement, remember?' She looked down at her hands, adding
in a low voice, 'I tried to tell you it wouldn't work,
but you wouldn't listen.'

Gerald Southall sucked in his breath, and to
Rowena's surprise gave her an awkward pat on the
shoulder. 'Sorry, lass,' he said gruffly, and shook
his head bewilderedly. 'Could have sworn it would
work out,' he said. 'You used to have a crush on
him once, didn't you?' he asked almost pleadingly.

Rowena swallowed. It was a bit late to tell him
that her adolescent crush on Sean had grown into
a heartbreaking love for the man she would soon
be parted from. 'Once,' she said in a tight voice,
'but that was a long time ago.'

Her father gave a deep sigh and walked over to
the window and stood gazing out. 'That's what
David said,' he remarked thoughtfully. 'But why
the devil didn't you come to me and tell me how
things were?' he demanded angrily.

'I tried,' Rowena replied, 'but as I said, you
wouldn't listen, you just went ahead and made the
arrangement.'

'But you went ahead and married him,' stuttered

her father with a trace of asperity in his voice. 'David said you'd got some fool idea that I'd cut him off without a penny if you backed out.'

Rowena nodded. 'That was part of it,' she conceded slowly, 'but it wasn't all,' she added.

Her father gave her a hard look. 'What else was there?' he demanded, and seeing her reluctance, ordered, 'Come on, out with it!'

Rowena sighed. 'You drew up a contract, remember?' she said gently.

Gerald Southall frowned, then gave an abrupt nod. 'What has that to do with it?' he asked impatiently.

She looked down at her hands again. 'Everything,' she replied quietly. 'Do you remember the terms?' she asked.

'Of course I do!' This time the impatience was more pronounced. 'I drew it up, didn't I?' he rasped. 'I didn't want any slip-ups. I wanted Tancred to know where he stood.'

Rowena's hands tightened together. 'Oh, he knew where he stood all right. He also knew where you stood if I backed out. I think,' she added with an ironic smile, 'that was something that you didn't take into consideration.'

Her father stared at her in amazement. 'Are you telling me he would have sued me?' he asked in a voice that showed his incredulity.

Rowena looked back at him steadily. 'For all you've got,' she replied dryly.

'The damned blackguard!' exclaimed her father. 'It was a gentleman's agreement!'

'Oh, come now, Father! Hardly that,' Rowena replied exasperatedly. 'You offer him a way out of his money problems, dangle a golden carrot in front of him—in other words, gave him the good news first, then the bad news. Think now,' she said gently. 'What would you have felt like? Of course he accepted, just as you knew he would, but you couldn't expect him to like it, any more than you could have expected him to sink his pride to the extent of——' She broke off lamely.

Her father coughed and looked away from her and out of the window again, then banged his hand down on the windowsill. 'I won't have it!' he said vehemently. 'I got you into this, and I'll get you out of it. Don't you worry, lass,' he said, reverting to the Northern accent that gave a hint of his feelings. 'I've just got to get a few details worked out, and when that's settled we're getting out of this snooty area. David's been telling me about a friend of his who lives in Kent. He's quite taken with the county. It's close to London, yet in the country. We'll see more of him too, like at the weekends. You'd like that, wouldn't you?' he asked her huskily.

Rowena was lost for words. She had never known her father in this mood, and it was all she could do not to cry, but somehow she managed a wan smile. 'I'd like that fine,' she said quietly.

It was at this tender moment that Sean chose to join them, and once again Rowena was annoyed at his intrusion, but her father welcomed it, it showed in his voice as he said in a satisfied air, 'Ah, just the man I want to see. I want my daughter released from the contract,' he demanded unceremoniously, and at Sean's raised brows, he continued, 'I'm a plain man, and see no reason to wrap it up. I made a mistake. I'm not putting the blame on anyone else's shoulders, and the least I can do is to make amends,' he declared grandly.

'That's mighty handsome of you,' Sean murmured, his lids hooded as he surveyed Gerald Southall.

Rowena closed her eyes. Why had Sean to come in at that precise moment? Another five minutes and her father would have gone. This conversation ought not to be taking place in her presence, but her father never saw the finer points of etiquette. 'If you'll excuse me,' she said quietly, and turned to go to her bedroom where she hoped she would not be able to hear the rest of this embarrassing conversation.

'You'll stay,' Sean ordered, proving that he could be as blunt as her father, and looked back at Gerald Southall waiting for him to go on.

Rowena's father glared at him, but did not countermand his order, and Rowena was forced to stay rather than antagonise either of the men further.

'There's nothing else to it,' declared her father. 'I want an end to it. You've no worries about losing out on the cash angle. I'm a man of my word,' he stated pompously. 'I'll still back you.'

Sean looked from him back to Rowena, who was vainly trying to dissociate herself from the whole business. She could not look at Sean, or at her father, but stared down at her hands now twisted together, and waited for Sean to accept the offer. It was that part of it that she hadn't wanted to hear, and what she would remember in the lonely days ahead of her.

'The trouble is,' Sean said slowly, but very distinctly, 'I can't accept those terms. Odd as it may seem I do have a certain amount of pride, even where the estate is concerned,' he added, underlining his meaning. 'If the marriage is annulled, so is the contract. I, too, am a man of my word. Whatever amount I have received from you will be paid back in full,' he said bluntly. 'That's the only condition I'll agree to.'

Rowena stared at him in horror. How could Sean possibly pay back all that money? He had gone ahead and ordered the start of the renovations, and even now the men were busy on the work. 'No!' she exclaimed quickly, before her courage deserted her. It wasn't Sean's fault that things hadn't worked out as her father had hoped. He had been honest with her from the start. He had known how it would be and had told her so. He would not go back on his word either, he would go to the money-lenders rather than do that. 'No,' she said again, and swallowed. 'I won't have my freedom under those conditions,' she said firmly. 'What's done is done, please leave it at that, Father.' She turned to Sean. 'Perhaps when you've had time to think about it, we can reach a compromise,' she said quietly.

Gerald Southall gave a snort of impatience as he strode towards the table where he had left his hat, and picking it up, looked across at Rowena. 'Well, I've tried,' he said irritably. 'And you think on, lass. The offer's a fair one. I'll say that for him. Use your sense and accept it.' He walked to the door. 'You know where to find me,' he said crossly before closing the door firmly behind him.

He had given up a little too easily for Rowena's liking and she surmised he was hurrying back for a council of war with David.

Now that Rowena was left alone with Sean, she was horribly embarrassed, and waited to hear him attempt to persuade her to follow her father's advice, and however much she wanted to, she simply could not, not under those conditions.

'Why did you say that?' Sean asked her quietly, cutting short her miserable musings.

'What?' she replied, not recalling what he was referring to.

Sean shook his head slowly. 'Now you know better than to ask that. You know very well what I'm talking about.' He gave a deep sigh. 'Oh, well, I suppose I shall have to make it plainer. Why did you refuse what your father said was a fair offer? You can have your freedom and it won't cost him a penny.'

Rowena blinked at him. He was not responding in the way she had thought he would, but then he never did, she thought crossly. 'Why do you think?' she replied crisply, showing him that she was not suffering under any romantic notions. 'I'll ask you a question,' she added. 'How on earth do you plan to reimburse my father?' she demanded.

His blue eyes met hers. 'So that's what you're worried about, is it?' he said musingly. 'Got a vision of me languishing in a debtor's prison, have you?' he taunted.

Rowena took a deep breath. 'Oh, well, if you can joke about it, I suppose I ought to accept the offer. Why should I care?' she added furiously.

'Why indeed?' Sean replied casually. 'What if I

tell you that I have ample funds to cover your father's loan, because that's what I intended it to be after inheriting a fortune from an old aunt whose existence, I'm ashamed to say, I'd completely forgotten about. Not entirely my fault, though—there's been no communication between her and the family since she eloped with her music teacher in the early thirties. It turned out that he made a fortune in the record business,' he added musingly.

Rowena stared at him, her brown eyes searching his as she tried to ascertain the truth of this, but it was a little too apt for her liking. 'You'll have to do better than that,' she said caustically.

Sean's blond brows rose haughtily, although there was a trace of amusement in his eyes. 'As a matter of fact, it's perfectly true,' he said calmly. 'I can assure you that I'd have made up a better story than that if I'd been wanting to deceive you.'

Rowena stared at him, with a nasty feeling that it was the truth. 'Why didn't you mention this to my father?' she asked, now highly incensed. 'You had no need whatsoever to make such a thing about refusing to accept his conditions and making me feel so awful—and I don't suppose Dad feels much better about it, either,' she added furiously.

'He needs a few jolts,' Sean replied unrepentantly. 'Do him good. He almost made a hash of things.'

'Almost!' exploded Rowena, glaring at him. 'Just how long have you known about this inheritance?' she demanded.

Sean's intense blue eyes met hers. 'About a

month,' he answered calmly, to her further fury.

'A month!' Rowena stuttered, as her mind went back over the time when she was organising the hunt ball, and all the running about she had had to do for him, and of what he had said when he had held her close on the dance floor, and all the time he had known! Her eyes widened. 'And you said nothing!' she exclaimed bitterly.

Sean shrugged his broad shoulders. 'I saw no point,' he replied carefully. 'I was quite happy as things were, or would have been, given time.'

Rowena turned away from his mocking eyes. He hadn't finished punishing her or her father was what he meant, she thought wretchedly, and how he must have enjoyed the situation, knowing that he could send both of them packing any time he felt like it. She turned abruptly on her heel and made for her bedroom. How she hated him—and to think she had tried to help him a few moments ago!

On reaching her bedroom she got her suitcase out of the wardrobe and slammed it on the bed, then started throwing her clothes into it.

'What are you up to now?' Sean queried lightly as he strode into the room.

She paused to glare at him. How dared he come into her bedroom! 'What does it look like?' she ground out furiously. 'I'm going back to where I belong.'

'I thought you'd agreed to stay,' Sean replied with a note of surprise in his voice that did not fool her for a single moment; he was having his little joke at her expense again.

'You know why I agreed,' she flung back at him, throwing everything into the case as fast as she could regardless of how it fitted in.

'I can see I shall have to teach you how to pack,' Sean commented maddeningly.

Rowena tossed another article in. 'I'm surprised you aren't helping me!' she said acidly. 'But don't worry, it won't take long.' There was a thud as a pair of shoes joined the motley collection in the case.

'I thought,' Sean went on, staring at the now piled-up suitcase as if mesmerised, 'that we might talk things over.'

'We've talked!' Rowena replied, wishing she could throw the hairbrush she had just thrown in the case at him.

'What exactly are you going to do?' he asked conversationally.

She straightened up and gave him a vague look. She had now got all in the case that she could get in, and she doubted whether she could close the lid. 'Do?' she repeated slowly, and her mind was now grappling with the problem of closing the case.

'I love that look of yours,' he said blithely. 'You don't quite focus, do you? It took me a while to realise that, and I used to think you were being deliberately provocative.'

Rowena took a deep breath. There was no coping with him in this mood. He was very pleased with himself, and no wonder, she thought. He had got rid of his unwanted lodger at last, and could afford to be expansive. She pulled the lid over the bulging suitcase and noted with exasperation that she would have to remove at least half the contents if she wanted to close the thing. 'I'm going home,' she said flatly. 'After that, I think I'll go to Paris with David. Anything else you want to know?' she queried, as she sat on the suitcase and tried jamming it down under her weight.

'Paris is out for a start,' Sean said firmly. 'Right now anyway, and certainly not with David. I don't trust those arty friends of his. Of course we could go later, when I've not so much on. Come to think of it, it will be an ideal place for a honeymoon— we never did have one, did we?'

Rowena paused in her weight-levering activities and stared at him. 'Are you mad?' she asked bluntly. 'You've got the wrong number. Diana's the one you ought to be talking to. Remember me?' she asked sarcastically. 'The grocer's daughter?'

'Ouch!' Sean winced and gave her a wicked grin. 'I don't seem to be getting through to you, do I? And why on earth should I be talking to Diana? Di's like a sister, we grew up together—not to mention saddling myself with Mrs Fisher as my mother-in-law,' he added with a grimace.

Rowena's lips clamped together. How cruel he was! He must know that Diana was in love with him. 'She's in love with you,' she said quietly, 'and don't tell me you didn't know, because I won't believe you,' she said accusingly.

Sean's blue eyes met her brown ones. 'She's always fancied she was,' he replied gently. 'I believe it's her mother's fault. She encouraged her, and tried her best to throw us together.'

'In that case I think you ought to make things quite clear to her,' Rowena replied steadily, thinking he ought to treat Diana as he had treated her; she would be under no illusions then.

'I thought you might help me out there,' Sean said quietly. 'You could move into my quarters for a start,' he added meaningfully.

'Of all the——' gasped Rowena. 'Do I look stupid?' she demanded. 'If you don't want Diana, then you'll have to look around for someone else. I'm out of the running!'

'Well, I thought a bird in the hand,' he replied with a wicked grin, as he walked steadily but surely towards her, 'and I'm quite satisfied with the wife I've got. I really can't be bothered to go all through that again.'

'Keep away from me, Sean Tancred!' Rowena gasped with a touch of panic in her voice. 'And get out of my rooms!'

'Our rooms,' Sean corrected softly. 'We'll both go after I've made certain of your co-operation,' he added significantly as he reached her and pulled her into his arms with a grip of steel that she could not break although she tried hard enough.

Rowena's resistance crumpled the moment his demanding lips found hers, and she went down in a kaleidoscope of rainbows, her doubts completely dispelled by the look in his eyes before his lips met hers.

A short while later as Rowena lay pliant in his arms, she remembered her family. 'Sean, what about David?' she asked, feeling a rush of remorse about forgetting them.

'Oh, I'll drop over there tomorrow,' Sean replied musingly, as he teased the corners of her lips. 'I think I'll ask both of them over to dinner, just in case they have any other stupid ideas about tearing you from my clutches, but I'm very much afraid they're going to be a shade too late,' he added softly, as his lips met hers again. 'Tonight belongs to us.'

SUPERROMANCE

Longer, exciting, sensual and dramatic!

Fascinating love stories that will hold
you in their magical spell till the last page
is turned!

Now's your chance to discover the earlier
books in this exciting series. Choose from
the great selection on the following page!

Choose from this list of great
SUPERROMANCES!

SUPERROMANCE

Complete and mail this coupon today!

- -

Harlequin Reader Service

In the U.S.A.
1440 South Priest Drive
Tempe, AZ 85281

In Canada
649 Ontario Street
Stratford, Ontario N5A 6W2

Please send me the following SUPERROMANCES. I am enclosing my check or money order for $2.50 for each copy ordered, plus 75¢ to cover postage and handling.

☐ #1 END OF INNOCENCE
☐ #2 LOVE'S EMERALD FLAME
☐ #3 THE MUSIC OF PASSION
☐ #4 LOVE BEYOND DESIRE

☐ #5 CLOUD OVER PARADISE
☐ #6 SWEET SEDUCTION
☐ #7 THE HEART REMEMBERS
☐ #8 BELOVED INTRUDER

Number of copies checked @ $2.50 each =	$_____
N.Y. and Ariz. residents add appropriate sales tax	$_____
Postage and handling	$_____ .75
TOTAL	$_____

I enclose_____.
(Please send check or money order. We cannot be responsible for cash sent through the mail.)
Prices subject to change without notice.

NAME_____
(Please Print)
ADDRESS_____
CITY_____
STATE/PROV._____
ZIP/POSTAL CODE_____

Offer expires April 30, 1982.

108563323